They were so different.

But why was she comparing him with Simon?

Melanie watched Gareth say something to the boy that brought a laughing response. He was so good with children. He should have children of his own. Maybe he had, for all she knew. Maybe he had once loved some woman enough to father her children.

At the thought of that something stirred inside Melanie, something she hadn't felt since Simon died, a feeling she'd thought she would never feel again. . .

Dear Reader

It's a children and animals month this time, as we have NO SHADOW OF DOUBT from Abigail Gordon, and TO LOVE AGAIN by Laura MacDonald dealing with paediatrics, and VET IN A QUANDARY by Mary Bowring dealing mainly with small animals — very appropriate for spring! We also introduce new Australian author Mary Hawkins, who begins her medical career at the opposite end of the spectrum with a gentle look at the care of the elderly. Jean and Chris are delightful characters. Enjoy!

The Editor

Laura MacDonald lives in the Isle of Wight. She is married and has a grown-up family. She has enjoyed writing fiction since she was a child, but for several years she has worked for members of the medical profession, both in pharmacy and in general practice. Her daughter is a nurse and has also helped with the research for Laura's Medical Romances.

TO LOVE AGAIN

BY

LAURA MACDONALD

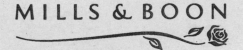

MILLS & BOON LIMITED
ETON HOUSE, 18–24 PARADISE ROAD
RICHMOND, SURREY, TW9 1SR

*First published in Great Britain 1994
by Mills & Boon Limited*

© Laura MacDonald 1994

*Australian copyright 1994
Philippine copyright 1994
This edition 1994*

ISBN 0 263 78564 5

*Set in 10½ on 12½ pt Linotron Plantin
03-9404-46345*

*Typeset in Great Britain by Centracet, Cambridge
Made and printed in Great Britain*

CHAPTER ONE

'I'LL be perfectly honest with you: if I'd been here for your interview I doubt you'd have got the job.'

'But I'm more than qualified.' Her anger mounting, Melanie Darby glared across the desk at Charge Nurse Gareth Morgan.

'I'm not talking about qualifications,' he replied calmly.

'Then what?' she demanded.

'I'm wary of taking on full-time staff who have such young children—part-time, maybe, but not full-time.'

'I find that remark sexist.'

'What do you mean?' There was amusement in his dark eyes now.

'Well, if I were a man it wouldn't matter one jot whether I had young children or not. . .would it?'

He shrugged. 'It would depend on the circumstances, but you're not a man, not a father, you're a mother; your children are only——' he glanced down at her file which lay open on the desk before him '—six and four, and in my experience, women with such young children suffer difficulties with routine. Why did you apply for this post, Mrs Darby?'

'Because I need the money,' she retorted.

'Quite.' He frowned slightly, drawing his dark eyebrows together into an uncompromising line. 'But what I meant was why this post in particular? Why paediatrics?'

'My previous work was with children.'

'Ah, I see, and when exactly was that?' He glanced down at the file again, but before he had chance to find the relevant information Melanie intervened.

'It was seven years ago, before my son was born, and, before you say it, yes, seven years is a long time away from the job, and yes, I know everything has changed.'

'I wasn't going to say anything of the sort, actually,' he replied mildly.

'And yes, I have done a refresher course. . . Oh!' She broke off as she realised what he had said. Suddenly she felt foolish; she had been convinced he had been about to mention the many changes that had taken place in the nursing profession in the last few years — the first major difference for Melanie being having a male charge nurse instead of a sister in control of the ward. She swallowed. 'I have every confidence that I shall soon pick things up again,' she said tightly.

'I have no doubts about that. As I said, my only doubts were over your domestic arrangements.' He closed her file, and Melanie stood up. 'But I'm sure you will have worked something out.'

'Of course.' She turned to leave the office, still seething.

'No doubt your husband is the co-operative sort and will do his fair share of the chores.'

Melanie stopped, one hand on the door-handle,

then without turning round she took a deep breath and said, 'My husband is dead, Charge Nurse Morgan; that is why I needed this job so badly.' Silence followed her statement, then without waiting for him to comment she put her head down and hurried from the room.

As she entered the ward she almost collided with an anxious-faced woman whom she recognised as the mother of a little boy who had been admitted that morning with a hernia.

'Oh, Nurse, I'm worried about Jeremy; he seems so hot.' The woman herself looked hot and flustered.

'Let's go and see, shall we?' Melanie led the way across the ward to a bed in the far corner and tried to shut from her mind the interview she'd just had with her charge nurse. It was her first day on the children's ward at St Mark's Hospital and she couldn't have got off to a worse start, but she was determined she wasn't going to let this attitude get to her; she had more than enough to think about as it was.

Jeremy, who was under observation, did indeed seem hot, and his chart showed that his temperature was slightly up, but it seemed to Melanie that anxiety could be the overriding factor with the four-year-old.

'Hello, Jeremy.' She bent down by the side of the bed. 'I've come to see Teddy—do you think I could have a look at his tummy?'

The little boy stared at her solemnly, his eyes huge, then shyly he pushed his teddy bear across the bed towards her. Gravely Melanie laid the bear on its back and began to test its furry stomach with her stethoscope.

Out of the corner of her eye she saw Jeremy sit up and lean forward with interest.

'Do you know, Jeremy, Teddy has got the same tummy ache as you,' she said after a while, and as the little boy digested that particular piece of information she went on, 'I shall need you to look after him for me.'

'Why?' Jeremy frowned.

'Why? Because I'm so busy looking after you and all these other children.' She looked around the ward and Jeremy followed her gaze, taking in the bright murals on the walls, the mobiles hanging from the ceiling and the other beds and cots. 'Do you think you could do that for me, Jeremy?'

He nodded shyly.

'Every time we take your temperature——' she held up a thermometer '—or test your chest, or even just give you a drink, I want you to do the same for Teddy—will you do that?'

He nodded again, and as Melanie straightened up she caught his mother's eye and smiled. The woman smiled nervously back and Melanie moved to the next bed, where an eleven-year-old girl was in traction following a riding accident.

'Everything all right, Katy?' She straightened the rumpled bedclothes.

The girl nodded. 'My dad's coming in today,' she said.

'That's nice—you'll be able to show him your tapestry.'

Katy nodded happily and Melanie moved away. She knew that Katy's anguish came as much from the recent break-up of her parents' marriage as from her broken leg.

A quick glance at her watch showed it was nearly time for the children's lunch, and she hurried to the nurses' station, which was at the far end of the main ward, with the intensive care unit and isolation beds beyond.

Jean Roper, who was acting sister, and Donna Marshall, a staff nurse like herself, were both in the nurses' station, and they looked up as she came into the room.

'What did he want?' asked Donna, who had been there when the charge nurse had called her into his office.

Melanie gave a wry smile. 'Only to tell me that he hadn't wanted me to get the job.'

'What?' Donna stared at her in amazement. 'He said that?'

'Yes.'

'But why?'

'Because I have young children, he seems to think I won't be able to cope with full-time work.'

'I hope you put him in his place,' replied Donna crisply.

'I did. I also accused him of being sexist.'

'You did what?' Jean's jaw dropped.

Melanie nodded and gave a grim smile. 'Yes, I

asked him if he would have worried if I'd been a man with two young children. Is he always such a chauvinist?'

Donna shook her head. 'Not usually. It sounds as if you just got off to a bad start with him.'

Melanie pulled a face. 'Yes, I suppose I have really.'

'He does have a point,' said Jean stiffly, and the other two turned to look at her in amazement.

'What do you mean?' demanded Donna.

'Well, let's face it, whenever we have full-time staff who have young children there are problems; there always seems to be something wrong—one of the children being ill or something—and if it isn't that it's some sports day or prizegiving. I happen to know it drives Gareth mad,' she ended smugly.

'Yes, you would know that, now you're in on everything,' Donna snapped.

At that moment a nursery nurse on the ward called out to Jean and she hurried away, leaving Melanie and Donna alone.

'Don't take any notice of her,' said Donna. 'This acting sister business has gone to her head. She's been driving us all up the wall—she thinks she's Gareth's right-hand angel.'

'I can see what they mean about it being irritating when staff are always going absent,' said Melanie. 'But I don't intend to be like that,' she added firmly.

'How old did you say your children were?' Donna began to pour orange juice into coloured beakers.

'Peter's six and Sophie's four.'

'So how will you manage?' Donna threw her a curious look. 'It won't be easy.'

Melanie sighed; she had already told Donna that she was a widow. 'I know that, but luckily the children go to the same school; Peter is in the juniors and Sophie still in the nursery school. My sister lives near by; she also has two children and we'll share things — school runs, that sort of thing. And they'll sleep at her place when I have to work nights. Don't worry, it'll work out all right.'

'Well, I hope it does for your sake.' Donna picked up the tray of beakers and walked into the ward, and as Melanie watched her she found herself hoping that things really would work out.

She had moved to Denehurst in Hampshire so that she could be near her sister, Jenny, whose husband was abroad in the Navy. Jenny was studying for the Open University, and the two of them had worked out a routine that would hopefully allow them to work and at the same time give the necessary care and time to their children.

She could have hoped for a more sympathetic boss, she thought as she made her own way back to the ward to assist with the meal trolleys that had just arrived from the kitchens. But there really wasn't much she could do about Gareth Morgan and his chauvinistic attitude, apart of course from making sure that she gave him no cause to fault her work or her timekeeping.

After assisting with the children's lunch she had two admissions to deal with, both for tonsillectomies the following day. One was a seven-year-old girl, Samantha, who had been in hospital before and knew exactly what it was all about, and the other a little boy called Richard, who was very apprehensive about the whole business.

Carefully Melanie explained to both Samantha's and Richard's mothers exactly what would happen the following day, then she encouraged the two children into the playroom to meet Lindsay, one of the ward's play therapists.

On returning to the ward she was surprised to find Gareth Morgan at Jeremy's bedside.

'Is there anything wrong?' she whispered to Donna, who was wheeling a trolley through the ward.

'I'm not sure,' Donna murmured out of the side of her mouth. 'The boy's mother still seems very anxious. It looks as if she's waylaid Gareth now. He's in a hurry, too; he has a meeting in five minutes.'

'I suppose I'd better see what the problem is,' said Melanie reluctantly.

Donna grinned, looped her dark hair back behind one ear, and trundled off down the ward with her trolley.

The charge nurse was sitting beside Jeremy's bed and appeared to be in deep conversation with the little boy.

As Melanie stopped at the foot of the bed Jeremy's mother looked up and gave her a nervous smile. 'I was worried about his breathing,' she explained. 'He seemed snuffly.'

Gareth Morgan glanced over his shoulder at

Melanie. 'Jeremy tells me you said that Teddy is to have an operation in the morning as well as him.'

Melanie swallowed. For the second time that day this man had made her feel foolish. 'Yes, that's quite right,' she admitted. 'Jeremy's looking after Teddy for me, aren't you, Jeremy?'

The little boy nodded gravely, and Gareth Morgan stood up. For the first time, Melanie was aware of his size as he towered above her. He must be well over six feet tall, she thought.

The charge nurse stood looking down at the little boy and his teddy, then he smiled, leaned over and touched the boy's head and, turning to his mother, said quietly, 'Don't worry about his breathing; the anaesthetist will be along to see him later this afternoon.'

'And Teddy?' asked Jeremy earnestly.

'Yes, and Teddy.' As the charge nurse straightened up he caught Melanie's eye, then with a brief nod he moved away down the ward.

'Isn't he nice?' Jeremy's mother stared after him. 'He's so big, but he's gentle and he's so good with the children.'

Melanie forced a smile. Gareth Morgan might well be good with the children; it was a pity he wasn't so understanding towards his staff.

When her shift was over Melanie changed out of her uniform, slipped on her coat and, pulling her black felt hat over her long fair hair, stepped out of the hospital into a bleak November afternoon. Turning up the collar of her coat, she hurried to the bus-stop, wishing for the umpteenth time that she hadn't found it necessary to sell her car. But it had been just one of the many economies she had been forced to make since Simon's death.

At least it was warm and dry on the bus, she thought as she watched the lighted shop windows in the high street. All the shops were packed with Christmas goods, a huge tree stood in the precinct, and a row of plucked turkeys hung in the butcher's shop window. Melanie was dreading Christmas. Last year had been awful, coming as it had only a few months after Simon's death, and she couldn't really see that this one was going to be much better. The children were looking forward to it, though, and she knew that for their sakes she had to make a supreme effort. Maybe it would be easier now that they were living near Jenny and her family.

If only she didn't still feel so cold and dead inside. Everyone had told her that in time it would pass. But it hadn't.

Mechanically she stood up as the bus stopped at Ferndale Road, returned the driver's cheery goodbye, stepped on to the pavement, and quickly walked the few yards to Jenny's house. Moments later she was greeted by the warmth of her sister's kitchen.

'How did it go?' Jenny, as dark as Melanie was fair, turned from the cooker, where she had just put the potatoes to boil for the evening meal.

'Not too bad.' Melanie dumped her bag on the kitchen table. 'Have the kids been all right?'

'Yes, they're watching the telly.' Jenny nodded towards the open door of the lounge, from where they could hear the sounds of a noisy children's game show. 'Cup of tea?'

'I'd love one.' Thankfully Melanie sat down and, kicking off her shoes, wriggled her toes. 'I'd forgotten how hard it is on the feet.'

'So do you think you're going to like it?' Jenny asked ten minutes later as the two of them sipped their tea.

'I hope so, but if I don't I'll just have to get on with it. Liking doesn't come into it.'

'That doesn't sound like you.' Jenny frowned. 'You used to love your work.'

'That was before.' Melanie sighed and pushed her hair back from her forehead. 'Everything's changed now.'

'Yes, I know,' said Jenny sympathetically, 'but that doesn't mean to say that you shouldn't like your work. What were the staff like on the ward?'

'OK.' Melanie wrinkled her nose. 'There's a staff nurse called Donna who seems particularly nice. . .'

'So what's bugging you?'

'What do you mean?' She glanced up quickly, then looked away.

'Well, something's obviously up. Come on, Melanie, this is me you're talking to. What's upset you?'

'It's more who than what,' she admitted, glancing up quickly as a little figure suddenly appeared in the open doorway.

'Didn't know you were here!' The little girl stared accusingly. Then she added in apparent triumph. 'Peter got told off at school today.'

'Hello, darling.' Melanie opened her arms to welcome her daughter, who suddenly hurled herself at her.

'So now we're getting somewhere. . .' Jenny went on, ignoring Sophie. 'Who exactly has upset you?' She stood up and carried her empty mug to the sink.

'It was just something the charge nurse said, that's all.' Melanie shrugged, pulled Sophie on to her lap, and buried her face in the mass of blonde curls. The little girl smelled of Marmite and baby shampoo.

'Well, are you going to tell me what it was?' Jenny had turned from the sink and was standing, hands on hips, watching her.

'Oh, it wasn't anything really. . .'

'Whatever it was, it's quite obviously upset you.' Jenny turned as her own daughter, Cassie, wandered into the kitchen and opened a biscuit tin on the worktop. 'Don't eat any more of those, Cassie,' she said sharply. 'You won't eat your dinner. . .'

'But I'm hungry. . . When *is* dinner?' Cassie gave an exaggerated sigh.

'Soon. . . So come on, Mel.' Jenny turned her attention back to Melanie again. 'What did she say?'

Melanie took a deep breath. 'It was a he, not a she—charge nurses are male,' she added in reply to Jenny's surprised expression.

'All right, then, what did *he* say?'

Melanie shrugged. 'Simply that he hadn't wanted me to get the job.'

'Why, for heaven's sake?' Jenny stared at her.

'Because of the kids. . . He doesn't think I'll cope.'

Jenny continued to stare at her, for once seemingly lost for words.

'He wasn't there when I went for the interview—I seem to remember someone saying he was away on a course. Anyway, it appears he isn't happy having full-time staff on his ward who have young children. He seems to have the impression the children will be ill most of the time, or that I shall keep needing time off. . . I don't know.' She shrugged. 'Maybe he has a point; maybe it will be too much——'

'Nonsense,' Jenny snapped. 'Of course it won't be too much. You'll just have to prove him wrong.'

'I just don't think he approves of working mothers,' Melanie said slowly. 'You know, a woman's place and all that—mothers should be with their children. . .'

'Chauvinist pig!' snorted Jenny.

'Whath a thauvinith?' asked Sophie solemnly.

'Nothing, darling.' Melanie smiled, hiding her face in her daughter's hair.

'Does he know you're a widow?' Jenny frowned and began folding a pile of clean washing.

'I don't think he did to start with—he must have missed it on my c.v.—but he does now. He made some remark about my husband helping me with the chores, and I told him.' As she thought of Simon, Melanie instinctively hugged Sophie a little tighter, then, easing the child from her lap, she stood up.

'This won't do,' she said briskly. 'We must get home, Jenny.' She turned towards the lounge. 'Peter!' she called, then, looking down at her daughter, she added, 'Get your coat, Sophie.'

'Mel,' said Jenny a moment later as she was helping Sophie with the toggles on her duffel coat, 'don't let this guy get to you, will you?'

Melanie shook her head. 'No, I won't. I didn't take this job for fun. I took it from sheer necessity, and it's going to take more than the likes of Gareth Morgan to stop me!'

'That sounds more like the Melanie I know.' Jenny chuckled. 'You know, I feel quite sorry for this guy, whoever he is. He's probably looked at you and thinks because you're blonde, petite and waif-like you are also fragile and helpless. Boy, is he in for a surprise when he finds out my little sister is really as tough as old boots!'

'Thanks, Jenny, thanks a million for those few kind words.' Melanie gave a wry smile and buttoned up her own coat.

'Mum, can I join the cubs? Jason Blackett goes.' She turned and found Peter at her elbow, and her heart gave a little jolt as it so often did these days as he gazed up at her with his father's steady grey stare. 'Can I, Mum?' he persisted.

'We'll see. . .' she promised.

'You always say that. . .'

'Later, Peter. . . We must get home now.'

★ ★ ★

The small modern semi in Winchester Close was in darkness as they approached. Melanie was fumbling in her bag for her keys when Peter suddenly clutched her arm. 'Look, Mum, there's a Suzuki jeep over the road,' he said.

She glanced over her shoulder, and in the light from an overhead street-lamp saw a red and white vehicle parked opposite.

'There's someone sitting inside,' Peter went on.

'Don't stare, Peter, it's rude,' she said. 'Come on, Sophie, hurry up.'

Pushing open the front door, Melanie flicked the light switch. Immediately the hall was suffused in a soft glow, and the warmth from the radiators welcomed them home.

'Mum, there's a man——' Peter was still standing on the doorstep.

'Peter, I told you not to stare,' said Melanie sharply. 'Come on inside. . .' She trailed off as she heard the sound of footsteps on the path.

Uncertainly Peter turned to her. 'Mum. . .' he began.

'It's all right, son.'

The deep voice with the Welsh lilt was instantly recognisable, and Melanie froze, one hand on the door-catch, as the footsteps stopped.

She looked up. 'Oh! It's you.'

'Yes.' He nodded. 'I need to speak to you. Could you spare me a few minutes?'

Helplessly she stared up at him. Had he come to

say she didn't have the job after all? That she wasn't suitable for the position?

'You'd better come in.' Her heart sinking, she stood aside as he stepped across the threshold into her home.

CHAPTER TWO

THE children, for once apparently subdued, hung back as Gareth Morgan followed Melanie into the lounge. He seemed to fill the room, and for a moment she found herself not only lost for words but also feeling very tiny beside him.

Sophie recovered first and bounced on to the settee, while Peter made a bee-line for the television, switching on the set and flicking from channel to channel with the remote control.

'Peter, put that off. . . Sophie, go and hang your coat up.' It came out sharper than she intended.

'I want to watch *Grange Hill*,' protested Peter, while Sophie climbed from the settee and stood at Gareth Morgan's feet, gazing up at him.

'You can watch the television later. Go and do your homework now.'

'I've done it; I did it at Aunty Jen's. . .'

'Peter. . .' There was a warning note in her voice, and her son must have detected it.

'All right,' he muttered, and headed for the door.

Sophie, however, wasn't so easy. Still staring up at the strange man who had invaded her home, she said, 'My nameth Thophie, whath yourth?'

'Sophie. . .' Melanie began warningly, and glanced

apologetically at Gareth Morgan. He was smiling, and she noticed how dark his eyes were.

'It's OK,' he said, then, crouching down so that his face was on a level with Sophie's, he went on, 'Hello, Sophie, my name's Gareth.'

'Why do you talk funny?' Sophie frowned, and Melanie wished the ground would open up.

'Because I come from Wales,' he replied solemnly. 'Why do you talk funny?'

'I don't!' She squirmed.

'Yeth, you do.' He imitated her lisp.

'I lotht my teeth,' she retorted.

'How?'

'I hit them on the thwing in the garden and they fell out.'

'So that's why you talk funny.' Gareth Morgan laughed, and unexpectedly Sophie laughed back. 'I want to talk to your Mummy,' he said solemnly. 'Would you like to go and find your brother?'

'What do you want to talk about?' Sophie demanded.

'Mummy's job.'

Melanie's heart sank even further. So she'd been right; that was why he'd come to see her.

'Mummy'th a nurth,' explained Sophie. 'I'm going to be a nurth. . .or perhapth I'll be a tank driver; I don't know yet.'

He laughed. 'I should stick to a nurse if I were you, Sophie; there aren't too many tanks around Denehurst. I'm a nurse,' he added, his smile widening as he saw the incredulous look on the little girl's face.

'But you're a man! You can't be a nurth!' She squealed with laughter, obviously thinking this was some sort of joke.

Melanie decided it was high time she intervened. 'Sophie, please go upstairs and get changed and talk to Peter for a while.'

Without a word Sophie obeyed her, apparently still bemused by what she'd just heard.

'She obviously doesn't know too many male nurses.' Gareth Morgan stood up.

'I'm sorry. She doesn't understand,' replied Melanie helplessly.

'She isn't the only one.' He gave a wry smile.

'What do you mean?' She frowned, suddenly curious at the cryptic note that had crept into his voice.

'I got much the same reaction back home in Wales when I first said I wanted to train to be a nurse.'

'Why was that? I know plenty of men who've done their nursing training.'

'Ah, but were their fathers and brothers all coal miners?'

She stared at him, then, seeing the gleam of amusement in his dark eyes, she found herself laughing. 'Oh, I see. . .' She trailed off, and in the silence that followed she waited for him to speak.

'You're wondering why I'm here?' He glanced round the lounge with its soft pastel walls and country-printed suite and curtains.

Suddenly she remembered her manners. 'Oh, please sit down. Can I get you anything to drink. . .?'

He shook his head. 'No, I won't keep you. I can

see you have plenty to be getting on with.' He nodded briefly towards the door. 'I've come because of what happened today on the ward.'

Here it comes, she thought miserably. He's going to say that he doesn't want to keep me on after my trial period is up.

'You see, I owe you an apology. . .'

Why didn't he just say it and be done with. . .? 'An apology?' Her head jerked up in surprise.

'Yes, when I made that remark about your husband I had no idea that you were a widow. It was insensitive and I'm very sorry.' He wasn't smiling now, and the glint of amusement had gone from his eyes.

Melanie found herself staring at him in amazement.

'Is anything wrong. . .?' He frowned.

'No. Oh, no!' Rapidly she tried to pull herself together.

'You look shocked. Have I said something else out of place?'

'No, of course not. It's just that. . .' She shrugged. What the hell? She might as well tell him. 'I thought you'd come to say that you didn't want me on your ward any more.'

'Why should you think that?' He looked incredulous now.

'Because of what you said today. I know you don't approve of working mothers——'

'It isn't that I don't approve of working mothers at all,' he interrupted. 'I just happen to think they have more difficulties than most, and, as I said, I had no idea you were on your own.'

'And it makes a difference now that you know I am?' She raised her eyebrows.

'Not really. I still don't think you'll find it easy working full-time with two young children to look after.' He glanced round the room as he spoke, his gaze coming to rest on Peter's school bag, which he'd dumped on one of the armchairs, and Sophie's coat draped over the arm.

'We'll manage,' she replied stiffly.

'Do you have a child-minder?'

'Not exactly, but my sister helps out.'

'Your sister?' He raised his eyebrows.

'Yes, she lives round the corner.' To her annoyance Melanie found herself explaining the arrangements she'd made. 'She takes the children to school when I'm on the early shift and collects them when I'm late.'

'So she doesn't go out to work?'

'Not exactly; she's studying with the Open University. Her husband is in the Navy, and when he's away her children will come here when I'm off duty, to give her the chance to study.'

Melanie was suddenly aware that he was staring at her in a kind of amazement.

'Well,' he said at last, his tone indicating the whole thing was beyond him, 'you seem to have it all worked out in theory—let's just hope it works when it's put into practice.'

'You sound sceptical, as if you don't think it will. We aren't the first, Mr Morgan; there are dozens of one-parent families these days who have to compro-

mise and do just what we are doing. It will work,
because it has to!' Her anger threatened to erupt.
What right did he have to question her domestic
arrangements?

He shrugged. 'We'll see. . .'

At that moment Peter stuck his head round the
door, the look he gave her visitor definitely suspicious.
'Mum? I'm starving.'

'I must be going.' Gareth Morgan used Peter's
intervention as his cue and moved to the door. 'You
have work to do and I want to get home to see the big
match.' He paused in the doorway and looked down
at Peter. 'I expect you'll be watching that tonight,
son, won't you?'

'I don't like football,' said Peter, looking at the
floor.

'Football? I was talking about rugby!'

'I don't like that either,' Peter replied without
looking up.

'You don't like rugby?' Gareth Morgan's voice rose
in disbelief, as if he'd been under the impression that
all small boys liked rugby. When Peter remained
silent, kicking at the edge of the carpet he went on,
'What do you like, then?'

Peter glanced up at Melanie. 'Collecting stamps,'
he said.

'Collecting stamps?'

Melanie's lips twitched at the look on Gareth
Morgan's face. 'Oh. I see.' He paused. 'Very nice
too. . .' he added. As he moved on to the front door a
sudden shout from above made him look up.

'I like rugby!' Sophie was sitting on the landing, her legs poking through the banisters, and her face squeezed in one of the gaps.

He laughed then, and Melanie noticed that his eyes crinkled at the corners. 'Yes, I dare say you do,' he replied.

He was still smiling as Melanie showed him out of the front door. He paused for a moment, staring at the steady drizzle that was falling, then turned up the collar of his waxed jacket. 'I'll see you tomorrow,' he said at last.

'Yes, all right.' She hesitated, her anger dissolved now. 'Thank you for coming, Mr Morgan,' she added.

'It was the least I could do—it was bothering me.' He turned away. 'Goodnight,' he called over his shoulder.

She watched as he walked down the path, then when he was halfway he stopped and turned. 'Oh, there was just one more thing.'

'Yes?'

'The name's Gareth.' He stood still for a moment, then with a little nod he went on down the path and began to cross the road to his jeep.

Melanie closed the front door and thoughtfully went back into the lounge.

'Who was that?' asked Peter. He still had the same suspicious look on his face, and Melanie smiled.

'Mr Morgan—he's the charge nurse on my ward,' she replied, picking up Sophie's coat from the chair.

'Why did he come here?' Peter demanded.

'He came to say he was sorry.' As she said it she

realised she was surprised that he should have done so.

'Sorry? Why, what did he do?' Peter glared at her.

'Hey, steady on.' She laughed and ruffled his fair hair, the indignant expression on her son's face reminding her once again of her husband. 'It wasn't anything he did; it was something he said.'

'What?' he demanded.

Melanie sighed. Peter quite obviously wasn't satisfied and wouldn't be until he got the truth.

'He made a remark about Daddy. . .'

'About Daddy? Did he know Daddy?' The grey eyes widened.

'No, darling, that was the whole point; he didn't know about Daddy. . .didn't know we were on our own. I don't think he thought I should be working with you and Sophie to look after. Afterwards, when he found out, he came to say he was sorry—it takes a man to do that, Peter.'

He scowled and she knew he was far from convinced, but she was saved from further argument by Sophie, who suddenly erupted into the room, carrying her pet rabbit.

'Sophie, don't bring Bengie in here—I've told you before. Take him back to his hutch. . .' She began to shoo her daughter out of the lounge and in the direction of the conservatory at the back of the house where the children kept their pets.

'Bengie'th hungry,' Sophie wailed.

'Will he come here again?' demanded Peter, who had followed them out of the lounge.

'Feed him, then,' Melanie said to Sophie, then turned to Peter. 'Who?'

'Him. That man.'

'I liked him; he wath a nith man, Gareth,' sighed Sophie. 'Ith he your friend, Mummy?'

'No, darling, he isn't my friend; he's my boss. And you needn't worry, Peter; I shouldn't think for one moment he'd be likely to come here again.'

'Good,' muttered Peter and disappeared back into the lounge.

'You haven't got any friendth, have you, Mummy?'

She looked down to find Sophie gazing solemnly up at her, the white rabbit still clutched tightly in her arms.

'I don't know many people here yet,' she admitted, 'but I soon will. Anyway, I've got you and Peter, haven't I?'

'I've got lotth of friendth. . . Luthy'th my beth friend. . .' The rabbit began to struggle frantically and Melanie quickly rescued it from Sophie's grasp and returned it to its hutch. When she turned round her daughter had scampered back to the lounge, from where Melanie could hear the sound of the television.

It was quite true what Sophie had said, she thought as she slowly went into the kitchen. She didn't have any friends—at least, not in Denehurst. All her friends were back in London—people who had been friends of them both in the old days, people whom if she thought about it, she rarely heard from now. They had all been marvellous at the time, of course, rallying round her, offering their support, but life had to go on, and people had their own lives to lead.

The evenings and the nights were the worst, after the children had gone to bed and she was alone with her memories. She longed for Simon then. She'd been angry when the shock had passed, angry that he should have left her to cope alone, to rear his children. Now the anger too had passed and she had been left with this terrible ache, deep inside, which she was convinced was going to remain forever.

Getting a job had been the best thing that could happen. She had been apprehensive about returning to nursing—so much had changed in the years she'd been away—but she had given herself a firm talking-to, gone on the refresher course, and had convinced herself she could do it.

What she hadn't bargained for had been having a boss like Gareth Morgan. Even though he had taken the trouble to apologise for his remarks, she knew she would constantly have to be on her toes where he was concerned if she was not to give him further cause for criticism.

The following morning she made sure she gave herself plenty of time so that she was on the ward five minutes before her shift started. It hadn't been easy. Peter had still been asleep and hadn't wanted to get up, and when they had finally got out of the house and were on their way to Jenny's Sophie had wanted to go back for her blue elephant. But somehow she had made it, and ten minutes after arriving she found herself in report as the night staff prepared to hand over.

Strangely she found she was apprenehsive at seeing Gareth Morgan, and wondered what his reaction would be. Would he mention in front of the others that he'd visited her? Or would he on the other hand not want it known?

She'd just reached the conclusion that he probably wouldn't be too keen on anyone else knowing, when he strode into the office and glanced round.

'Good morning, everyone,' he said, and for the second time Melanie noticed how dark his eyes were.

There were general murmurs of, 'Good morning', from the rest of the staff, then to Melanie's dismay his gaze came to rest on her.

'All well, Melanie?'

'Yes. . .yes, thank you,' she mumbled.

'Did Sophie enjoy the rugby?'

'Er—I'm not sure. That is. . .' She floundered, aware of glances from the rest of the staff.

'At least the right team won.' He smiled, the dark eyes crinkled at the corners, and Melanie quickly looked away.

There were four children for Theatre that morning: Jeremy, with his hernia, a baby for circumcision and the two children for tonsillectomies.

'Jeremy's mother is as anxious as ever,' said the night sister, glancing at her notes. 'She will be staying here during Jeremy's treatment, but it seems that little we do or say can alleviate her fears. She had hardly any sleep last night, and the problem, of course, is that her anxiety is transferring itself to Jeremy.'

After report, Gareth outlined the duties for the day. 'Jeremy's pre-op care plan must include the highest level of reassurances and explanation for both mother and child,' he stressed to the assembled staff.

'Melanie,' he went on, and she looked up quickly, surprised that he should be singling her out, 'I'd like you to take care of Jeremy both pre- and post-op and to help his mother to cope.'

'Yes, all right.' She nodded, but just before Gareth went on with the rest of the day's work plan she was aware of a speculative glance from Donna.

And later as they left the office and made their way back to the ward Donna said, 'Gareth seems to have changed his tune towards you.'

'What do you mean?' She played for time, pretending she didn't understand what Donna was driving at.

'Well, only yesterday you said he'd had a go at you, and you were accusing him of being the biggest chauvinist of all time. Now, this morning, he couldn't seem to take his eyes off you, and you were blushing like a schoolgirl.'

'Don't talk such rubbish,' she protested. 'He simply asked me to care for Jeremy, that's all. He had to ask someone to do it; it just happened to be me.'

'Hmm.' Donna sounded far from convinced. 'What did he mean about rugby?'

'Oh, nothing much.' She felt herself colouring under Donna's curious gaze.

'And who's Sophie?' Donna clearly didn't intend to let it go.

'My daughter.'

'Your daughter? Oh, of course, I'd forgotten that's her name.' Donna nodded, then a slow frown crossed her features. 'But how does Gareth know your daughter?' she asked curiously.

Melanie swallowed and, turning away, opened the door of the linen cupboard and began to pull out a pile of clean sheets. 'He doesn't really know her,' she muttered. 'He's only met her the once, last night. . .'

'Last night?' Donna's eyes were like saucers, and Melanie sighed. It looked as if she was going to have to give some sort of explanation, otherwise heaven knew what could be misconstrued from what had, after all, been an entirely innocent event.

'Yes,' she said firmly. 'Gareth came round to apologise for upsetting me. He met my children, and my daughter, Sophie, who's a terrible tomboy, told him that she liked rugby.'

'So are you saying that Gareth Morgan actually came round to your house?'

'Yes, why? Is there anything wrong?' Melanie became aware that Donna was staring at her in astonishment.

'No, there's nothing wrong. It's just amazing, that's all.' Donna began shaking her head as she too took sheets from the cupboard.

'Why? I don't understand. What's so unusual about that?'

'If you only knew just how many have tried to get

Gareth Morgan's attention and failed miserably. . .'
Donna chuckled '. . .while you, you're in the place
for one day and you have him falling over himself to
apologise for some silly remark. . . I've got to hand it
to you, Melanie; you're certainly a fast worker. . .'

'Just a minute, Donna; you've got it all wrong,' she
protested. 'There's absolutely nothing like that!'

'Oh, come on, Melanie. . . I wasn't born yesterday.' With a laugh Donna moved away down the
ward to Katy's bed, leaving Melanie staring after her
in dismay.

CHAPTER THREE

TRYING to put her conversation with Donna firmly out of her mind, Melanie made her way down the ward to Jeremy's bed to prepare him for his operation.

Winter sunshine streamed through the high arched windows, melting the frost patterns on the panes of glass and flooding the ward. Already the play therapist had organised some of the children into making paper-chains from strips of gummed paper, while from the radio at one end of the ward a pop group reminded everyone it was Christmas time again.

'Hello, Jeremy, it's me.' Melanie stopped beside his bed and smiled. 'I've come to get Teddy ready to have his tummy mended.'

'What's that on your pinny?' The little boy was staring at the PVC apron that Melanie was wearing over her blue uniform.

'This is my dinosaur pinny,' she replied, and with a laugh she pointed to the brightly coloured pictures of a family of dinosaurs. 'See, this is the mummy dinosaur, the daddy is going off to work, and the little one is playing with his toys, just as you do, Jeremy.' She glanced up as she spoke. 'Where's your mummy?'

'In there.' Frowning, Jeremy pointed to the guest-room where his mother had spent the night.

The door was tightly shut, and Melanie hesitated

for a moment, then she said, 'Tell you what, Jeremy, would you like to start cleaning Teddy up for me? We'd better not put him in the bath, because his fur will get wet, but take one of these——' she pulled a moist wipe from a packet in his locker and handed it to him '——and make sure you get him really clean.'

'Where are you going?'

'I'm just going to have a word with your mummy.'

There was a muffled response from inside the guest-room when Melanie knocked, and when she opened the door and popped her head round she was dismayed, but not entirely surprised, to find Jeremy's mother with red, swollen eyes.

Quietly she went right into the room and closed the door behind her. 'Hello, Rosemary. . .you don't mind if I call you Rosemary, do you?'

The woman shook her head and sniffed.

'I just thought I'd pop in to see you, because I know exactly how you must be feeling this morning.'

The woman threw her a withering look that implied she doubted that Melanie had any idea how she was feeling.

Ignoring the look, Melanie said, 'I felt exactly the same when my little girl broke her arm and had to have it set in Casualty.'

'You've got children?' Rosemary had turned to the wash-basin, but she paused and looked back at Melanie.

'Yes, I have two: a boy, Peter—he's nearly seven—and a daughter, Sophie, who's four. She's a real tomboy, always in trouble — she broke her arm falling off a wall in the back garden.'

The woman was silent for a moment, then she sighed. 'I know it's stupid, but I can't help it. . . I have this fear of hospitals, you see. . .'

'It isn't stupid at all,' said Melanie gently. 'A lot of people feel the way you do.'

'I'm convinced something will happen to him — that he'll die under the anaesthetic. . . I couldn't bear it. . . I know I mustn't let him see me like this; that's why I shut myself in here. . . But he'll be wondering where I am. . .' Her voice broke and she turned helplessly away.

'The doctor did explain everything to you about the operation, didn't he?' Melanie put her arm round the other woman's shoulders.

'Yes, last night when I signed the form.' Her eyes filled with tears again. 'I wish I hadn't signed it now.' She pulled away from Melanie.

'You don't mean that,' said Melanie firmly, 'because if you hadn't signed Jeremy could have found himself in all sorts of trouble in the future, and I know you wouldn't want that.'

When Rosemary didn't reply, Melanie went on, 'Tell you what, why don't you come and help me to get Jeremy ready for his op? We'll get him bathed and nice and comfortable, then after he's had his pre-med, you could read him a story.'

Still the woman hesitated, fighting her fears, and in the end Melanie held out her hand. 'Come on. He'll be all right — really he will — but he'll be much better if you're there with him.'

At last Rosemary took a deep breath, then she nodded. 'All right,' she said, 'I'll try and help; I suppose it'll be better than just sitting around waiting and wondering.'

'Of course it will — and I'll be glad of your help. Don't forget, we have two of them to get ready.' Melanie opened the door and stood back for Rosemary to precede her.

'Two of them?' She frowned.

'Yes, Teddy's going too.'

'Of course, I'd forgotten.' She smiled then, her tension eased, if only slightly.

As they approached Jeremy's bed Melanie saw that Gareth had come into the ward and was in conversation with Jean. For a brief moment she recalled what Donna had said about Gareth falling over himself to apologise to her, and she felt her cheeks grow warm. Donna had made it sound as if the charge nurse had been after her, had even implied that she had set out to attract him herself, and that couldn't be further from the truth. Not that he wasn't attractive, she thought as she and Rosemary stopped beside Jeremy's bed, but in a rugged sort of way, not her type at all.

At that moment he looked up and saw her.

'Ah, here she is,' he said, then he must have seen the reflective, slightly quizzical look on her face, because he frowned.

'Everything all right, Staff?' he asked before allow-ing his gaze to flicker to Jeremy's mother.

'Yes, everything's fine,' replied Melanie firmly, pulling herself together. 'We're just going to get Jeremy bathed.'

'We wondered where you'd got to,' said Jean. 'There's a lot to get through this morning.' Her acid tone suggested that she thought Melanie had been wasting time.

'I know that,' replied Melanie, 'but first things first. Right, Jeremy——' she looked down at the little boy '——is Teddy nice and clean?'

Jeremy nodded, looked anxiously at his mother, then when he saw she was smiling said, 'I told Teddy he mustn't have a drink.'

'That's quite right; in fact I think we'll give Teddy a badge the same as yours.' Melanie pointed to the 'I must not eat or drink' badge that was pinned to Jeremy's Postman Pat pyjamas.

'I can see you have everything under control here,' said Gareth with a laugh, 'so I'll leave you to it. See you later, Jeremy, old man.' He winked at the little boy and moved away down the ward.

Melanie looked up and was in time to see a strange expression flit across Jean's features. She had no time to pursue it, though, as Jeremy's needs claimed her full attention.

She encouraged Rosemary to bath her son and dress him in his theatre gown while she made up his bed ready for his return from Theatre.

'Now,' she said when Jeremy was lying on the top

of his bed covered with a single blanket, 'I'm going to go and get some medicine. While I'm gone I want you and Mummy to make a gown for Teddy.' As she spoke, Melanie handed Rosemary a white hand towel and a couple of large safety-pins.

In the treatment-room she found the acting sister preparing a dressing trolley. Jean Roper, several years older than both Melanie and Donna, was a tall, thin woman with large, expressive eyes, and had her dark hair cut in a short, severe style.

Since Melanie's arrival, of all the staff on the ward, Jean had been the least friendly. She didn't turn from the dressing trolley, so Melanie got quietly on with preparing the syrup for Jeremy's pre-med. It was several minutes later when Jean spoke, and it came so suddenly that it made Melanie jump.

'That child seems to be taking up a lot of time.'

When Melanie looked up it was to find Jean standing, hands on hips, watching her, a disagreeable curl to her mouth.

'The mother is very nervous and it's transmitting to the child——'

'I know that,' Jean snapped impatiently. 'They're all the same, but we don't have time to mollycoddle them all.'

'I wasn't mollycoddling Jeremy.' Melanie felt her cheeks grow hot. 'Gareth asked me to help ease the situation, and that's exactly what I've done.'

'Oh, Gareth asked you, did he?' mimicked the other woman, turning the trolley sharply and almost colliding with Donna.

'What's up with her?' Donna looked over her shoulder as Jean clattered off down the ward to Katy's bed.

Melanie shook her head. 'I'm not sure, really. She said I was spending too much time with Jeremy, but Gareth did ask me to didn't he? You heard him, Donna.'

'Yes, I heard him.' Donna grinned. 'But you have to use your own discretion. Gareth is brilliant at his job, but I've never known another charge nurse — or sister, for that matter — quite like him.'

'What do you mean?' Melanie stared at her.

'He spends hours with the kids and expects everyone else to do the same.'

'However does he find the time with a ward to run?'

'That's the whole point; there isn't time, but he's so soft-hearted that he comes in when he's off duty to see the kids. Did you see the older ones playing with those puzzle books this morning?'

Melanie nodded.

'Well, Gareth bought those for them when he collected his morning paper — he's always doing things like that.'

'That's great, but it still doesn't give Jean the right to say what she did to me. . .'

'Don't take too much notice of Jean.' Donna laughed. 'She's been on this ward longer than any of us, and she'll be peeved because Gareth particularly asked you to look after Jeremy and not her.'

'But——'

'Jean's always fancied her chances with Gareth; she hates it when he seems to favour anyone else.'

'But he wasn't favouring me,' protested Melanie. 'Everyone seems to have got quite the wrong idea. Why, only yesterday he was as good as saying he didn't want me on this ward. He simply gave me a duty to perform. I don't know why Jean can't just accept that.'

'Wait till she knows about last night — that'll really set the cat among the pigeons. . .' Donna gave a wicked chuckle.

'I explained about that. . .' Melanie protested.

'I know.' Donna laughed knowingly, then, growing serious, she said, 'Forget it.' Glancing down, she added, 'Is that Jeremy's pre-med?'

Melanie looked at the phial in her hand. 'Yes.'

'I've come to get Samantha's and Richard's.' Donna chuckled again. 'That Samantha's a one! I've had to watch her; she's been frightening poor little Richard to death with stories about what they do in Theatre.'

Melanie turned away, still troubled by what had happened.

By the time she got back to Jeremy's bed, however, she had tried to put it out of her mind.

With some gentle persuasion from his mother, Jeremy took his fruit-flavoured pre-med syrup, then Melanie produced a dinosaur book from the library shelf in the playroom and Rosemary began reading to her son and his teddy bear.

Melanie busied herself with other duties in the ward, and was just assisting Donna with theatre preparations when the porters arrived for a suddenly very frightened Samantha.

Reassuring her young patient, Donna escorted Samantha to the theatre, and Melanie returned to Jeremy's bed.

Rosemary looked up as she approached. 'He's fallen asleep,' she whispered.

'I thought he would.' Melanie smiled down at the little boy, who lay peacefully with his thumb in his mouth and his teddy tucked into the crook of his arm.

'Has that little girl gone down for her operation?' Rosemary nervously glanced at Samantha's empty bed.

'Yes.' Melanie nodded. 'It'll be Jeremy's turn next; would you like to come down with us?'

'To the theatre?' Rosemary's eyes widened with fear.

'No, not right into the theatre, just to the anaesthetic room,' explained Melanie.

'I don't know. . .'

'Tell you what. . .' Melanie deliberately kept her tone cheerful. 'You come down with us, then if you don't want to go in I'll stay with Jeremy while he has his anaesthetic, and you can wait outside. Then we'll come back to the ward together. You'll need to be here when Jeremy comes round. It'll be you he wants to see, not me.'

'All right.' Rosemary took a deep breath but still looked very apprehensive, and Melanie knew she was going to have her work cut out if she was to keep her calm.

She didn't have too long to think about it, though, as only moments later the porters were back for Jeremy.

'Now here's a nice little lad.' Tom, the elder of the two men, beamed at Rosemary. 'Oh, hang about; looks as if we have two to move here, Steve.' He grinned at his young assistant and pointed to Jeremy's teddy bear while Melanie checked the identification band on Jeremy's wrist, his medical notes and his treatment card.

As he was lifted on to the trolley the little boy opened his eyes.

'It's all right, Jeremy,' said Melanie. 'It's time to go for a ride.'

'And Teddy?' he murmured drowsily.

'Yes, and Teddy.' She glanced at Rosemary. 'You walk alongside and hold his hand,' she added.

When they reached the theatre Melanie indicated for Rosemary to sit in a chair outside the anaesthetic room. 'I won't be long,' she promised. As Melanie moved through the double doors into Theatre the last thing she saw was Rosemary's anguished face, and her heart went out to her.

She remained with Jeremy, holding his hand while his anaesthetic was administered, then when he was asleep Sister wheeled him into the theatre. Melanie caught a brief glimpse of Mr Charles, the paediatrician, in his green gown and mask before she slipped outside to join Rosemary again.

The woman was sitting on a chair in the corridor,

and she jumped as Melanie appeared. 'Is everything all right?' she gasped.

'Everything's fine,' replied Melanie, then realised that Rosemary was staring at Jeremy's teddy, which she held in her arms.

'Why have you brought that out with you?'

'So that I can put a plaster on its tummy before Jeremy wakes up, that's all, Rosemary.'

The woman continued to stare, then suddenly her shoulders sagged and she laughed. 'My God, it just shows the state I'm in, doesn't it? I'd actually come to believe that bear was having an op as well!'

'I'm glad we've been convincing.' Melanie laughed too, then, touching Rosemary's arm in a sympathetic gesture, she went on, 'Come on, let's get back to the ward. We just about have time for a cup of tea.'

Rosemary stood up and they began to walk up the long corridor.

They had almost reached the ward when Rosemary suddenly spoke. 'I don't know what I would have done without you,' she said quietly.

Melanie smiled and threw her a quick glance, noticing how white and strained she looked.

'I think I would have gone completely to pieces,' she went on. 'I only have Jeremy, you see. . .since his father left us. . . We only have each other, and if anything happened. . .'

'I know how you feel. Ours is a single-parent family as well.'

'You're divorced?' Rosemary threw her a curious look.

Melanie swallowed. 'No, I'm a widow.' It still hurt her to say it, still sounded as if she were talking about someone else.

'Oh! But you're so young!' Rosemary looked shocked. 'In fact I was surprised when you said you have children; you hardly look out of your teens yourself.'

'It's kind of you to say so.' Melanie laughed, then pulled a face. 'But believe me, there have been times in the last year or so when I've felt about a hundred.'

'I'm so sorry.' Rosemary looked genuinely concerned, then quietly she said, 'Was he ill, your husband?'

Melanie shook her head. 'No, he was killed.'

By this time they had reached the ward, and she was further aware of Rosemary's still shocked expression. 'I think,' she said firmly, 'that we're both ready for that cup of tea.'

She led the way into the nurses' kitchen and filled the kettle, then, leaving Rosemary to put milk into the cups, she hurried into the treatment-room and cut a piece of sticking-plaster from a reel. Removing the protective backing, she stuck the plaster firmly to the teddy bear's furry stomach, then made her way back to the kitchen. She was about to push the door open when she heard Gareth's voice from inside and realised he was talking to Rosemary.

'She's been absolutely marvellous,' she heard Rosemary say. Melanie paused, instinct telling her they were discussing her. 'I don't know how I would have got through without her,' Rosemary went on. 'I know how busy she is, but nothing has been too much trouble.'

'We aim to please,' Gareth replied. 'I'm only glad it was Melanie who was available to help you.'

Suddenly she felt good and, taking a deep breath, she cleared her throat and, pushing open the door, walked into the kitchen. Gareth was perched on a stool, watching Rosemary as she made the tea. He looked up quickly at Melanie and, maybe because his words had made her feel good, she felt her heart miss a beat. When he saw the bear in her hands Gareth smiled.

'Well, that's Teddy ready and waiting,' she said, aware her voice sounded a little shaky. She glanced at Rosemary, then back at Gareth. 'We were going to have a cup of tea — will you join us?'

'I'd like to——' he glanced at the fob watch on the front of his white jacket '—but I'm expecting a doctors' round in a few minutes.'

'Oh?' Melanie had moved forward and begun to pour the tea, but she looked up quickly, wondering if Gareth needed her on the ward.

'It's OK.' He seemed to read her mind. 'You stay with Rosemary.' He stood up, and with a smile and a nod to both women he left the room.

Rosemary watched him go, then with a sigh and a wistful smile she turned to Melanie.

Suddenly Melanie panicked. From the look on Rosemary's face she knew that she too was going to start jumping to conclusions about herself and the charge nurse. She handed Rosemary her tea, and in a desperate attempt to steer the conversation in another direction she said, 'Have you done your Christmas shopping yet?'

For one moment Rosemary looked startled, then she shook her head. 'I haven't been able to think of anything except Jeremy coming in here. I shall have to get cracking now, though, otherwise we won't be having a Christmas.' She paused. 'What about you?'

Melanie laughed and shook her head. 'I'm nearly as bad. We've just moved house and I'm still sorting everything out. We did find the tree decorations the other night, much to my daughter's relief.'

They had barely finished their tea when Donna put her head round the door. 'Jeremy will be back shortly,' she said.

'Already?' exclaimed Rosemary. 'I had no idea it would be so quick.'

'Come on.' Melanie drained her mug. 'We must get his bed ready and be there to receive him.'

They jumped to their feet and hurried on to the ward, where the doctors' round was already under way.

Melanie checked that the oxygen and suction beside Jeremy's bed were working properly and that a vomit bowl and tissues were at hand. She also made sure that everything was ready to maintain four-hourly observations of pulse and respiration.

Samantha was back from her tonsillectomy and was crying noisily. Rosemary threw an anxious glance in the direction of the child's cubicle.

'It's OK, Rosemary, Donna is with her,' reassured

Melanie, then, glancing up, she said, 'Here comes Jeremy now.'

The little boy was lifted into his pre-warmed bed, and as Melanie began his observations Gareth and the group of doctors and students stopped at the foot of the bed.

'This is Jeremy,' explained Gareth. 'He has just come back from Theatre where he's had a femoral hernia repair. Is all well, Staff Nurse?'

'Yes, everything is fine, thank you.' Melanie finished recording Jeremy's pulse and respiration readings on to his chart and handed them to the senior registrar, Dr Jubhati. He studied the readings, then murmured something to the paediatrician, Susan Lineham.

Rosemary looked anxiously from one to the other, but the registrar merely smiled and nodded.

'Thank you, Staff,' said Gareth, and moved on to Samantha's bed, pushing the trolley of patient records before him, the group of doctors in his wake.

'Is everything all right?' Rosemary swung round to Melanie.

'Yes, everything is fine.'

'They never tell you anything, do they?'

'They probably don't want to worry you.'

'They worry me more by not saying anything. . .' Anxiously Rosemary turned back to her son. 'He looks so pale. . . Are you sure he's all right?'

'Positive.' As Melanie answered, the little boy began to stir and open his eyes. Swiftly she walked round the bed and drew his mother forward so that hers was the first face he saw.

'Hello, darling.' Tenderly Rosemary smoothed her son's hair from his forehead.

'My tummy hurts. . .' The child began to whimper, and his mother looked up.

Carefully Melanie checked the wound site and observed a small amount of blood on the dressing. 'I'll give Jeremy something for his pain,' she said. 'While I go and get it, what I'd like you to do, Rosemary, is to sit beside him, hold his hand, and make sure he doesn't try to get up.'

Jeremy made a good recovery during the rest of the day, and just before Melanie finished her shift Gareth called her into his office.

He was sitting at his desk and he indicated for her to close the door. 'I just wanted to say how well you've done with Jeremy.' He leaned back in his chair and, picking up a pen, began toying with it. For a fleeting moment Melanie got the impression he was faintly embarrassed, as if he was recalling the last conversation they'd had in this office only the day before. 'And with his mother,' he added as an afterthought. 'She hasn't stopped singing your praises.'

'It was nothing, really, all in a day's work.' Melanie felt her cheeks grow warm.

'Even so. . .' He shrugged. 'It's not everyone who has the patience or even the knack of dealing with that sort of thing.'

'Maybe it's something to do with being a mother myself,' she replied quickly. 'It does have its compensations, you know.'

'*Touché*,' he said softly and smiled up at her.

CHAPTER FOUR

'Mum!'

'What is it now, Peter? We're going to be late if we don't hurry up.' Melanie stood at the bottom of the stairs and shouted up to her son, who was still in the bathroom.

'I've got a sore throat.'

Her heart sank. Surely Peter wasn't going to go ill on her — not at this time in the morning.

'I had it when I woke up.' He came to the top of the stairs and peered over the banisters.

'All right.' She sighed and began to climb the stairs.

'It's only a little bit red, Peter,' she said moments later, after she'd inspected his throat. 'And your glands aren't swollen. I really don't think it's bad enough to stay off school,' she added doubtfully.

'I suppose not.' He gave an exaggerated sigh.

'Mummy, I've lotht my play thooes,' yelled Sophie from her bedroom.

'All right, all right, I'm coming.' Helplessly Melanie looked at her son, who had adopted a very woebegone expression. 'Tell you what, Peter, go to school today and we'll see how your throat is tonight. . . All right, Sophie! I said I was coming!' she added as another howl from her daughter rent the air.

Somehow she got them all out of the house, but this part of the day was by far the worst for Melanie, and when she reached Jenny's house, where she usually just dumped the children and ran for the bus, she felt honour bound to explain about Peter's sore throat.

'I'll keep an eye on him,' promised Jenny. 'And I'll mention it to his teacher. Now go, or you'll miss your bus.'

'But. . .do you think——'

'Just go, Mel. You don't want that bloke thinking you can't cope, do you?'

She fled at that, but when she reached the corner it was only to see the bus pulling away from the stop. There was a ten-minute wait for the next bus, and by the time it arrived Melanie was fretting and fuming, knowing there was now no way she would be in time for report.

She had been on the ward for nearly two weeks, and during that time she hoped she had proved she could more than cope with her life as a working mother. She had even begun to establish a good working relationship with Gareth, but now it looked as if she could blow it all by being late.

By the time she reached the hospital, had changed into her uniform, and arrived on the ward, it was to find that report had indeed started and the staff were all in the office.

With a sinking heart she tried to slip unobtrusively into the room, but, as luck would have it, the door-catch clicked and everyone looked round.

The night sister glared at her and Gareth raised his eyebrows.

'I'm sorry,' she mumbled. 'Sorry I'm late.' She sank into a chair and was aware of a sympathetic glance from Donna and a smug look from Jean.

The report included details of Jon, a cystic fibrosis sufferer who had been admitted the previous day with severe breathing problems, and a six-year-old girl, Kirsty, who had been admitted as an emergency during the night with suspected menengitis and who was being nursed in isolation.

The theatre list for the day consisted of one boy suffering complications from a fractured femur, an appendicectomy and a eight-year-old girl for the removal of her adenoids.

As they left the office after report, Donna threw Melanie a sideways glance. 'Everything all right?' she asked quietly so that the others wouldn't hear.

'I think so.' Melanie nodded and sighed. 'It was Peter; he woke up with a sore throat, but it didn't seem bad enough to keep him away from school. Anyway, I had to stop to mention it to my sister and it was enough to make me miss the bus.'

'I don't know how you cope,' said Donna. 'It must be hell. I'm glad I don't have kids.'

'It's OK when everything goes smoothly — it's only when something like this happens that I start to panic.'

'What would you do if the children were really ill?' asked Donna curiously.

'I'd have to rely on Jenny. There's nothing else I

could do.' Melanie shrugged, then glanced over her shoulder. 'Can we change the subject? Gareth's coming. I don't want him to know what happened.'

Donna nodded and began sorting through the day's clean bed linen.

'Melanie, we have an emergency coming in.' Gareth paused beside them, then looked from Melanie to Donna then back to Melanie again. 'Is everything all right?' he added.

'Yes, everything's fine,' replied Melanie quickly.

'Good.' He hesitated. 'I just thought there might be some sort of problem.'

'No, nothing.' She shook her head, hoping he wouldn't mention her being late for report. 'An emergency, you say?'

'Yes.' Gareth was still frowning, but he carried on, 'A baby with suspected pyloric stenosis, referred by its GP. Are you familiar with pyloric stenosis, Melanie?'

'I know a bit about it.' She nodded. 'The main symptom is projectile vomiting after a feed, isn't it?'

'That's right,' Gareth agreed. 'Apparently this infant is dehydrated. The parents are accompanying it. Will you do the admission, Melanie? Donna, I'd like you to prepare the two boys for Theatre.'

The baby arrived ten minutes later, a little boy, barely six weeks old. The first thing that struck Melanie was how young the baby's parents looked. The mother, her long hair falling over her face, looked exhausted, while the father seemed little more than a schoolboy and didn't look as if he'd even started shaving.

The baby was fractious, crying and chewing his fist, and his mother Tracey was almost beside herself with worry.

'He can't keep nothing down,' she said as Melanie took the baby from her. 'Every feed he has, he brings it back up.'

'I know, Tracey,' Melanie replied. 'But he's here now and the doctors will be able to put things right for him.'

'They'll think it's our fault, won't they?' Tracey shot a worried look at her boyfriend. 'It isn't our fault, is it, Sean?'

Sean shook his head. 'No, we did everything we could. Just when we thought we'd got a feed into him, he'd chuck it right across the room. Honest, Nurse, it isn't our fault.'

'It's all right, nobody's going to think it's your fault,' said Melanie, then, raising her voice above the baby's wailing, she went on, 'It sounds as if Daniel has a blockage in his stomach—but we'll be able to put it right for him—'

'A blockage?' Tracey too raised her voice. 'What do you mean? He hasn't swallowed anything he shouldn't.'

'No, I don't mean that sort of blockage.' Melanie passed the baby to one of the nursery nurses who had just come into the office. 'Thanks, Bridget,' she said to the girl. 'Look after baby Daniel while I fill in his admission forms, will you? Dr Lineham is on her way up to the ward to see him.' As Bridget lifted the baby to her shoulder and began gently rubbing his back, Melanie sat down at the desk and turned back to the parents. 'This blockage,' she explained, 'would be something he was born with.' She took her pen from the pocket of her uniform. 'Now I want you to tell me all about Daniel—his feeds, his weight, how many times he fills his nappy. . .everything you can tell me that will help the doctor.'

Susan Lineham arrived just as Melanie finished the admission, and they all followed her into the treatment-room, where she carried out her examination of baby Daniel.

'Because he's had no nourishment he has become dehydrated,' the doctor explained to Daniel's parents. 'I'm going to set up a drip,' she went on, 'and the best place in which we can do this in such a young baby is through a vein in his scalp.'

'I can't watch this.' Tracey became very distressed and began to cry.

'You'd better come with me,' said Melanie gently, then, glancing at Sean, she added, 'Do you want to come as well?'

Sean shook his head. 'No, I'll stay,' he replied shakily.

Melanie took Tracey down the ward, intending to let her wait in the visitors' rest-room, but as they passed the open door of the office Gareth looked up from a report he was writing.

'Problems?' he asked.

'Not really,' replied Melanie. 'I was just taking

Tracey to the rest-room to wait while Daniel has his infusion.'

'Why don't you come in here, Tracey, and keep me company for a while?' Gareth pushed aside his pile of papers. 'I've had enough of this lot for one day.'

'Tracey's very worried about the blockage that baby Daniel may have,' said Melanie, seeing Tracey's doubtful look at the prospect of sitting with the charge nurse.

'In that case I'd better explain what it's all about.' Gareth stood up and lifted a book from the shelf behind him.

By the time she left the office Gareth and Tracey were poring over coloured pictures and diagrams while Gareth patiently explained the nature of pyloric stenosis.

On her arrival back in the treatment-room Melanie found that Dr Lineham was ready for her to assist with setting up the intravenous infusion.

Carefully she shaved a small area of the baby's head, just enough to expose the vein into which Dr Lineham was able to introduce the cannula. Immediately afterwards Melanie inserted a naso-gastric tube so that the contents of the baby's stomach could be aspirated.

Throughout it all, Sean stoically watched every procedure that was carried out on his baby son. 'He will be all right, Nurse, won't he?' he asked anxiously as Melanie carried out a pulse and respiratory check.

'Yes, of course he will. He's a brave little chap and we'll keep a very close eye on him.' Melanie glanced up as the door opened. 'Ah, here comes his mum,' she said as a fearful-looking Tracey came into the room, accompanied by Gareth. 'Just the person we wanted, eh, Sean?' Melanie smiled, then, glancing at Tracey, she explained, 'Sean is making sure Daniel doesn't pull his drip out, but I would like you to clean baby's mouth with a cotton bud. Could you do that for me, Tracey?'

'There you are, Tracey,' said Gareth. 'You were only saying a moment ago that you felt useless, and wished you could do something to help.' He turned to Melanie. 'Oh, Nurse, there's a phone call for you.'

'For me?' Startled, she looked up.

'Yes.' Gareth nodded. His expression remained impassive, giving nothing away regarding the nature of the call or his reaction to her receiving a call on the ward. 'You can take it in my office. I'll stay here,' he added as she glanced uncertainly down at the baby.

'Thanks,' she muttered and hurried from the cubicle.

In Gareth's office she picked up the receiver from the desk. 'Hello?' she said tentatively. Intuition had already warned her what she might be about to hear, and she half expected to hear Jenny's voice on the other end.

'Oh, hello, Mrs Darby. It's Eileen Roach here.'

'Mrs Roach?' She frowned; why would the children's headmistress be phoning her? She knew to phone Jenny if anything was wrong. . .unless, maybe, something was very wrong. Instinctively she gripped the receiver more tightly. Ever since she'd had the dreadful news about Simon she seemed to have a sense of foreboding about everything, especially where the children were concerned.

'I thought I should ring you, Mrs Darby. Peter doesn't seem at all well. He said he told you he had a sore throat this morning.'

Was that a reprimand to her for sending him to school?

'And now he appears to be running a temperature and is complaining of a headache. I really think he should be at home.'

'Yes, of course, Mrs Roach,' she said. 'Have you telephoned my sister?'

'Yes, Mrs Darby. I tried several times, but there's no reply.'

'I see.'

Where was Jenny, for heaven's sake?

'Shall I tell Peter you are on your way to collect him?'

'Er—yes, yes, of course, Mrs Roach. Thank you for letting me know.'

'That's perfectly all right, Mrs Darby; it's what we're here for.'

There was a click from the other end of the line, and Melanie stared at the receiver. What could she do? Perhaps she could try and ring Jenny again. Maybe her sister was there now. Maybe the headmistress had been ringing the wrong number.

Quickly she glanced through the office door into the ward. The treatment-room door was closed, indicating that Gareth was still in there.

Without giving herself time to think about it, she dialled Jenny's number. She heard the ringing tone and found herself counting the number of rings. Ten, eleven, twelve. Where was her sister? Thirteen, fourteen——

'Is something wrong, Melanie?' The voice broke into her thoughts, and she spun round to find that Gareth had come silently into the office behind her.

'What? Oh, no, nothing's wrong. . . I was just trying to ring my sister. . . She doesn't appear to be in. . .' She trailed off and realised he was staring intently at her.

'There is something wrong. What is it?' He closed the door behind him, and Melanie knew she was trapped. She didn't want to tell him, didn't want him to think there was a problem, didn't want him to think she couldn't cope, so that he could say, I told you so.

'Is it the children?' he asked quietly.

She hesitated, playing for time, then, 'It's Peter,' she admitted at last.

'What's wrong?'

'That was his headmistress on the phone. He's not feeling well.'

'Was he all right this morning?'

She swallowed. 'He had a sore throat.'

'Should he have gone to school?' He was frowning again.

'Oh, don't you start!' she cried. 'His headmistress implied that I should have kept him at home.'

'And do you think you should have done so?' His voice was calm, quiet, but he raised his eyebrows.

'Well, obviously now I realise that's what I should have done,' she replied heatedly. 'But at the time he didn't seem too bad. Honestly, Gareth, if children were kept home every time they complain of some little thing, none of them would ever go to school.'

'OK, all right.' He held up his hands as if to fend her off.

She continued to glare at him for a long moment, then she sighed and looked away. 'I'm sorry,' she muttered. 'It's just that I was feeling guilty enough as it was without you pointing out my responsibilities to me.'

'What is the headmistress going to do about it?'

'She wants someone to go and fetch him. . .'

He glanced at the phone. 'Your sister?'

'As I said, she doesn't appear to be in. I can't understand it. . .'

'You can hardly expect her to be there all the time just in case something happens,' he said mildly. 'She's probably gone shopping or something.'

'Maybe I should try again,' she muttered, her irritation growing, but this time with him and not Jenny.

'Maybe you should go and get Peter yourself and take him home,' he said quietly.

She stared at him, then looked up at the clock on the office wall. 'But I have another couple of hours to go yet.'

'I expect we'll cope without you. Do you have transport?'

'No.' She shook her head, thinking miserably how she would have to get two buses to the school, then another to her home.

'In that case I'll run you to the school,' he said smoothly.

Her head jerked up sharply. 'Oh, no, I couldn't possibly expect you to —— '

'Why not? I can arrange cover. I'm off duty anyway in half an hour. Get your coat and we'll get going.'

He sounded so decisive that she knew there was little point in further protest and, if she was honest, she was relieved to have a lift. Moments later when she came out of the staff-room she found Gareth waiting for her. He had taken off his white coat and was wearing his waxed jacket.

'Ready?' he asked, his gaze roaming over her long navy coat and the felt hat that covered her fair hair.

She nodded, and together they began to walk towards the corridor.

'Hey, where do you think you two are off to?' The sudden shout from the kitchen made them both turn. Donna stood in the open doorway, a look of astonishment on her face.

'Slight crisis,' Gareth replied. 'Julie Marder's taken over, and I know you and Jean will cover for Melanie.'

Jean must have heard her name, for she stuck her head out of a cubicle. 'What's going on?' Her eyes narrowed suspiciously as she caught sight of Gareth and Melanie in their outdoor clothes.

'I'm not sure.' Donna gave a wicked chuckle. 'But at a rough guess I'd say these two are eloping, and a good thing too. It's about time we had a bit of romance around here.'

Melanie turned to flee, but not before she'd caught sight of the furious scowl on Jean's face.

Gareth was smiling when he took his seat beside her in his Suzuki jeep. 'I reckon this could give them all something to talk about on the ward,' he said as he turned on the ignition.

'What do you mean?' She threw him a startled glance.

'It's not every day I disappear in the middle of the day with one of my nurses.' He chuckled. 'I hardly make a habit of it, you know.'

'Oh, no, of course not.' Suddenly she felt silly. Then she threw him an anxious glance. He was staring straight ahead, concentrating on joining the traffic, and it struck her once again how attractive he was, in a very virile, masculine sort of way, with his dark good looks and his Welsh charm. As if he sensed her watching him he turned his head, and as his eyes met hers she looked quickly away.

'Maybe I should.' He chuckled.

'Should what?' She felt uncomfortable that he had caught her watching him, almost as if he had read what she had been thinking.

'Make a habit of this sort of thing—what did you think I meant?'

'You don't think they will?' She ignored his last

remark. 'Think anything, I mean?' An image of Jean's furious expression was still in her mind.

'I expect so,' he replied breezily. 'That lot would read something into anything; they love a bit of gossip. Still, if they're talking about us, they'll be giving some other poor devil a rest. Besides, it doesn't bother me one iota. . .' He threw her a sidelong glance as they pulled out into the flow of traffic. 'Does it bother you?'

'Oh, no,' she said quickly.

He was silent for a moment, then he said, 'So you wouldn't mind if everyone did think we had something going between us?'

'What?' She threw him another startled glance, but his expression was poker-straight.

'That wasn't what I meant at all,' she protested. 'What I meant was. . .' She floundered, searching for the right words to explain just what she had meant, then she heard him chuckle.

'It's all right,' he said. 'I know what you meant; I was just teasing.'

She fell silent and looked out of the window at the brightly lit shop fronts, feeling decidedly foolish again. What must he think of her? She had quite forgotten how to flirt, it had been so long.

She wasn't sure how or when it happened, but suddenly she realised she had became very aware of him in the close proximity of the cab of the jeep. Had he been flirting with her? Would she mind if he had?

'What will you be doing for Christmas?' he asked suddenly.

'Oh, we'll just be at home,' she said, thankful that he had changed the subject.

'Will you spend it with your sister?'

'Probably Boxing Day, but Christmas Day she is going to her in-laws, so it'll be just me and the children. What about you? Is it home to Wales?'

'No, I'm on duty most of the time.' He paused. 'Don't you have any other family?'

'Oh, yes, I have my parents,' she replied.

'And won't you see them at Christmas?'

She shook her head. 'No, they live in Spain. My father has been ill recently and they aren't able to travel this year.'

'So it really will be just you and the children?'

She nodded and fell silent again, having to fight the lump that had suddenly risen in her throat as she thought of other Christmases when Simon had been alive — happy family times full of love and laughter. She knew she would have to make a supreme effort this year for the children's sake, but she was dreading it.

When they arrived at the school, Gareth parked the jeep outside the gates and switched off the engine. 'I'll wait here,' he said as she opened the door.

'Oh, you needn't wait,' she said quickly. 'It was very kind of you to bring me, but we can get the bus home.'

'Don't be silly; you won't want to take the little lad on a crowded bus if he's feeling ill. Go and fetch him.'

His tone indicated that he would take no argument, so after only a moment's hesitation Melanie hurried into the school. She found Peter in the rest-room which adjoined Mrs Roach's study.

'Ah, Mrs Darby, I'm so pleased you were able to get away, I really do think Peter should be at home.' Was there an accusing note in the headmistress's voice, Melanie wondered, or was it she who was becoming paranoid?

To her dismay Peter did indeed look flushed and his forehead felt hot.

'I thought Aunty Jen would come,' he said as she helped him into his coat.

'Aunty Jen wasn't in,' explained Melanie.

'Does that mean we have to get the bus?'

'No, I had a lift here.' They took their leave of Mrs Roach, and as they stepped into the playground Melanie wrapped Peter's scarf warmly around his neck and across his mouth.

'Oh, goody,' he mumbled through the scarf, clearly pleased that they didn't have a long wait at a cold bus-stop.

When they walked through the school gates, however, and he caught sight of the Suzuki jeep parked by the kerb, a frown creased his forehead. 'What's he doing here?' he said.

'Mr Morgan brought me here to pick you up,' said Melanie, recognising the rebellious note in her son's voice. 'It was kind of him; I'm very grateful.'

Peter didn't reply, and as they approached the jeep Gareth got out and came round and opened the rear passenger door.

'Hello, son,' he said. 'Not feeling so well today?

Never mind, get yourself up in here and we'll soon have you home in the warm.'

Still Peter didn't answer, although Melanie suspected he would be pleased by the prospect of a ride in the jeep. For some reason it just seemed to be Gareth he didn't like.

Peter's silence continued during the drive back to Winchester Close. Gareth drew up outside the house and turned to look at Melanie. 'Maybe it's a good thing you're off duty now for a couple of days,' he said.

She nodded ruefully. 'I was thinking the same thing. . .' She opened the door and climbed from the jeep just as Gareth came round to open the passenger door.

'Thank you very much for bringing us home,' she said, looking at Peter, who had climbed from the jeep and was standing on the pavement, kicking the kerb. 'It was very kind of Mr Morgan, wasn't it, Peter?' she said pointedly.

Peter nodded without looking up, and helplessly Melanie turned back to Gareth. 'Er—would you like to come in. . .?' she asked, looking up at him.

'Mum!' Peter tugged at her sleeve.

Gareth looked down at Peter, then at Melanie. 'I don't think so,' he said quietly. 'You get indoors and see to this young man.'

'All right, if you're sure, and thanks again.'

She knew he was watching them as they walked up the path, then as she fumbled for her key in her handbag he climbed back into the jeep. As she opened the front door and they stepped into the hall he raised his hand in farewell.

Suddenly, unreasonably, she didn't want him to go and found herself wishing he had come in with them and perhaps shared a pot of tea. But before she could raise her hand in response Peter had pushed the front door firmly shut.

'Peter! Why did you do that?' She stared down at him in exasperation. 'Mr Morgan will think us very rude.'

Peter shrugged and began unwinding his scarf. 'I don't like him,' he said flatly.

'But why?' She frowned. 'I don't understand. He's only been kind towards you; why should you dislike him?'

'I don't know. I just do.' Peter pulled off his coat and draped it over the newel post before trailing upstairs.

CHAPTER FIVE

WITHIN half an hour Melanie managed to get Jenny on the phone and explain what had happened.

'Oh, God! I'm sorry,' her sister said. 'I was only next door, having a cup of tea with my neighbour.'

Weakly Melanie leant against the wall. Was that all it had been? 'Oh, well,' she heard herself say, 'it doesn't matter now; it was just one of those things.'

'So what happened? How did you get to the school?' asked Jenny.

'Gareth Morgan gave me a lift.' As she said it she knew she would have difficulty making Jenny understand.

'Gareth Morgan! Not chauvinist man himself?'

'Yes, none other.' Melanie smiled in spite of herself.

'Oh, I say, that makes it even worse. I really am sorry, Mel. Was he very angry that you had to leave work?'

'No, as a matter of fact he wasn't.' She hesitated and glanced up the stairs, aware that Peter was probably listening to every word she was saying. 'He was very good about it. Actually I'm beginning to think I misjudged him when I called him a chauvinist,' she added as an afterthought.

'But he did say he didn't want you to have the job because you were a working mother, didn't he?'

'Y. . .e. . .s,' she admitted slowly.

'Well, in my book that makes him a chauvinist of the first order.' Jenny sounded indignant. 'He's quite obviously one of those men who thinks a woman's place is in the home. . . Anyway, that's not the issue at this moment. What you're saying is that you have Peter there with you. How is he?'

'His temperature is up slightly and he still has a sore throat. I think he's probably starting one of his colds, but if he's any worse in the morning I'll call the doctor, just to be on the safe side.'

'What about Sophie?'

'She's all right.'

'No, what I meant was——' Jenny sounded impatient, '—is she with you or is she still at nursery school?'

'Oh, I see.' Melanie smiled as she realised her mistake. 'No, Sophie isn't with me.'

'In that case I'd better be getting down the road to meet her.'

'Thanks, Jen.'

As Melanie replaced the receiver Peter called from upstairs. 'Mum, who's going to look after me if I don't go to school?'

'I will. I've got two days off.'

'Oh, good,' he replied.

The following day Peter had all the symptoms of a head cold, with a runny nose, tickly cough and streaming eyes. Melanie persuaded him to stay in bed. She spent the morning catching up on household chores and the afternoon reading to him from one of his favourite adventure books.

By the next day he was over the worst of his cold, and he got dressed at lunchtime and came downstairs. They spent part of the afternoon sorting out and writing Christmas cards.

'Aunty Jen will be here with Sophie soon.' As Melanie glanced at the clock the doorbell rang.

'Oh, they're early!' She jumped to her feet and hurried to answer the door.

'I didn't expect you yet. . .' she began as she pulled open the door, then the words died on her lips. Instead of her sister and Sophie, Gareth Morgan stood on the step.

'Oh, it's you!' She stared at him in amazement, aware that her heart had lurched crazily at the shock of seeing him there.

'Yes, it's me.' He smiled, the dark eyes lighting up. 'Who were you expecting?'

'My sister, with Sophie,' she said faintly.

He was wearing a cream Aran sweater over black cords, and the wind had ruffled his dark hair. He smelled of some woody, earthy aftershave, and the sheer size of him seemed to fill the doorway.

'I came to see how Peter is,' he explained.

'Oh, he's much better, thank you. It was only a cold after all, but he was a bit poorly there for a while.'

'Can I see him?'

He was staring at her, a glimmer of amusement in those dark eyes, and she suddenly became very aware that she had no make-up on, her hair was screwed up in a topknot, and she was wearing her old black leggings and a sloppy sweater. She suddenly felt about twelve years old, but in spite of her humiliation she found it difficult to look away. Then to her confusion she realised he was waiting for an answer and she didn't know what he had said.

'I'm s-sorry. . .' she stammered. 'What did you say?'

'Peter. . . Can I see him?' There was more than a hint of humour now in the dark eyes and around his mouth, as if he found her confusion amusing. 'I have something for him,' he added, as if extra persuasion might be needed.

'Oh, yes, yes, of course.' Somehow she managed to drag her gaze away from his. 'Please, come in.' She knew she sounded breathless. She stood aside for him to enter the hall, closed the front door behind him, then put her head down so that he wouldn't see her embarrassment and hurried into the lounge ahead of him.

'Peter, you have a visitor,' she said quickly.

Peter looked up from the table where he had been sticking stamps on her pile of Christmas envelopes, and Melanie saw the frown that creased his forehead as he caught sight of Gareth.

'Hello, Peter, how are you feeling today?' Once again Gareth's frame seemed to fill the room.

'All right. . .' Peter glanced at Melanie, then grudgingly added, 'Thank you.'

'I wondered if you'd like these. . .' Gareth put his

hand into the back pocket of his cords and drew out an envelope. 'It's only some stamps. I know you said you collect stamps, and you may well have these, but I thought you might like to have a look.' He opened the envelope and emptied the contents across the table.

Peter leaned forward, and Melanie was amused to see how interested he was, in spite of the fact that he'd said he didn't like Gareth.

'I haven't got that one——' Peter stabbed a finger at one of the stamps '—or that one, but I've got the complete set of those. D'you want to swap?' He frowned up at Gareth, apparently less suspicious of someone who seemed to know his stamps.

'I'll go and put the kettle on,' said Melanie in relief. 'I expect you'd like a cup of tea, Gareth.'

'I'd love one,' he said quietly. He looked up at her, and as their eyes met he smiled.

For the second time in the space of a few minutes she felt her heart lurch, and she turned and hurried into the kitchen, suddenly feeling ridiculously happy. She couldn't explain why she felt pleased that Gareth seemed to have broken through Peter's resentment, but she was. She often worried that Peter had little male company, surrounded as he was by females— even his cousins, Jenny's children, were girls.

Jenny arrived with Sophie just as Melanie was setting out the cups.

'Have you got visitors?' her sister asked. 'There's a jeep outside.'

'Gareth Morgan's here.' Melanie lowered her voice,

and as her sister stared at her in surprise she was furious to find her cheeks growing warm.

'What's he doing here?' demanded Jenny indignantly.

'It's all right, really. He's just come to see how Peter is. . .'

'Oh, Gareth! He'th a nith man.' With a whoop of joy Sophie dumped her school bag and made a bee-line for the lounge.

'Well, at least someone seems to like him,' remarked Jenny drily.

'Would you like a cup of tea?' Melanie asked, hoping her sister would refuse, and hating herself for it.

'Er. . .' Jenny hesitated and glanced at her watch. 'I should be getting back, really. . .but yes, all right, just a quick one. I'd quite like to meet this self-opinionated guy,' she added, pulling a face.

'Jenny——' Melanie swallowed as she filled the teapot and set it on the tray '—please don't say anything, will you?'

'What do you mean?' Jenny stared at her.

'About what he said—you know, working mothers and all that.'

'Well. . . I——' Jenny began, a mulish expression on her face.

'Jen, please.' Melanie protested. 'He does happen to be my boss, and he could make life very difficult for me. I know he was insufferable to start with, but he has been very helpful since, especially where Peter is concerned.'

'OK, point taken.' Jenny gave an exaggerated sigh and helped herself to a digestive biscuit from the plate that Melanie had put out. 'I won't say anything. . . but I'm still intrigued,' she added with a hint of mischief in her tone.

Melanie threw her sister a worried glance, then picked up the tray and led the way into the lounge.

Gareth's dark head and Peter's fair one were close together as the two of them pored over Peter's stamp album while Sophie sat hunched up on the settee, a scowl on her face.

Peter was the first to look up. 'Mum, these stamps are brill. I didn't have hardly any of them. . . Hello, Aunty Jen,' he added as an afterthought.

'Well, it's very kind of Mr Morgan to think of you.' Melanie glanced at Gareth as she set the tray down. 'Gareth, this is my sister, Jenny.'

'Hello, Jenny.' He straightened up and held out his hand.

'I've heard a lot about you.' Jenny unashamedly allowed her gaze to roam over him.

Melanie, about to pour the tea, found herself waiting, teapot poised, wondering what would come next. Her sister was always outspoken and had never been renowned for her tact.

'Really?' There was surprise in Gareth's tone, and just as Melanie resigned herself to the fact that he was about to question the statement, with possible disastrous consequences, the moment was saved by Sophie, who suddenly bounced off the settee.

'It'th not fair.' She pouted. 'Gareth ith my friend. Why hath he come to thee Peter?'

Gareth smiled and crouched down so that he was on a level with her. 'I came to see Peter because he isn't very well, but I came to see you too.'

She stared suspiciously at him, as if she wasn't really convinced, then as if she'd suddenly remembered something important she solemnly announced, 'I'm an ath.'

'What did you say, Sophie?' Melanie looked up sharply, a cup of tea in one hand.

'An ath, in the Chrithtmath play. I'm an ath, and Paul'th an ockth.'

'Oh, I see,' said Melanie in relief as both Gareth and Jenny smiled.

'I thought you would have been an angel with your hair,' said Jenny, leaning forward and affectionately ruffling her niece's curls.

'I didn't want to be an angel!' Sophie protested indignantly. 'Angelth are thoppy. I wanted to be an ath and wear a mathk.'

'I'm sure you will make a lovely ass,' said Gareth solemnly.

'Will you come and watch me?' demanded Sophie.

His hesitation was only momentary. 'If I possibly can, I will,' he promised. 'That is,' he added, 'on condition you come and watch me play rugby.'

'Ooh, yeth. . .' breathed Sophie.

Taking the cup and saucer that Melanie offered him, Gareth turned to Peter. 'Are you in a Nativity play as well, Peter?'

Peter nodded and carried on sorting his stamps.

'And what part are you playing?' Gareth persisted. 'A shepherd? Or one of the kings, perhaps?'

'The angel Gabriel,' muttered Peter gloomily.

'He's clever, I'll grant him that,' said Jenny thoughtfully as they stood in the lounge window and watched Gareth climb into his jeep and drive away.

'What do you mean?' Melanie frowned and threw her sister a quick glance.

'Well, he obviously knows that in this case the way to a girl's heart is through her kids.'

'What in the world are you talking about?' Melanie turned from the window and glared indignantly at her sister.

'Him—Mr Wales.' Jenny grinned and jerked her head in the direction of the street. 'He obviously fancies his chances. . .'

'Hith name'th Mithter Morgan, not Mr Mithter Waleth,' said Sophie suddenly.

Melanie spun round; she had thought that Sophie had gone upstairs with Peter. 'Sophie, go and find Peter for a while, will you? I want to talk to Aunty Jen.'

'But I want to thee Thcooby Doo——'

'Now, Sophie.'

'All right!' Sophie gave a dramatic sigh and rolled her eyes, then she flounced out of the room and they heard her thumping up the stairs.

'She's getting out of hand.' Melanie sighed, running her fingers through her hair in distraction.

'She needs a father.' Jenny grinned. 'And that

brings me back to what I was saying about your Welsh friend.'

'I know what you were implying, but it's absolute rubbish,' said Melanie hotly.

'Is it?' Jenny raised her eyebrows. 'You can't deny he's showing a lot of interest in the children, and, as I said, that would be one sure way of getting to you.'

'That's not the case at all,' she retorted. 'You're forgetting, Jen, he works with kids, and from what I've seen so far on the ward he's very good with them—a natural. In fact he loves them, so you can't go reading anything into the fact that he's shown a bit of kindness to my two.'

'Yes, but honestly! Stamp-collecting!' Jenny lowered her voice so that the children wouldn't hear. 'If stamp collecting's his hobby, I'll eat my hat. Now rugby. . .yes, that's a different matter; I can quite easily imagine him covered in mud, heaving and grunting in the midst of a scrum. . . Sticking stamps in an album? No way.'

'I still don't see why he couldn't do both,' began Melanie defensively. 'Besides, what's wrong with stamp-collecting, for heaven's sake.'

'Nothing. . .there's nothing wrong with stamp-collecting. . .' Jenny was laughing now. 'It just isn't him, that's all. You mark my words, it's a ploy, and if I'm not very much mistaken he definitely had a way of looking at you.'

'Now you are talking nonsense!' To hide her confusion Melanie picked up the tray and headed for the door.

'What do you know about him?' Jenny followed her into the kitchen.

'Not a lot,' she replied firmly. 'Only that he comes from a Welsh mining community and that he's a charge nurse.'

'He's not married?'

'Not as far as I know.'

'Well, that's a start anyway.'

'A start to what, Jenny?' She banged the tray down on the draining-board in exasperation. 'Honestly, you're being absolutely impossible. I'm not looking for a relationship, and even if I were I don't think I'd be bothering with Gareth Morgan. From what I've heard I'd just be wasting my time.'

'Ah, so you do know more about him.' A speculative gleam had come into Jenny's eye.

'Only what Donna, one of the other nurses on the ward, told me.'

'Which was?'

'That there have apparently been several women interested in him since he's been at the hospital, but that he's shown no interest in return. There's one in particular—a woman called Jean, who's on our ward—who seems to think of him as her personal property. I wouldn't be too keen to tangle with her.'

'Can't say I blame her. Let's face it, he's gorgeous . . .all that simmering Welsh passion. . . But, more to the point, are her attentions returned?'

'I honestly don't know, Jenny. . .and besides, aren't you forgetting something?'

'What's that?' Jenny raised innocent eyebrows.

'I don't want that sort of involvement with anyone. It's too soon. . . I'm simply not ready.'

Her sister remained silent for a moment, then when she spoke her tone was gentle.

'It's well over a year, Mel. You're young, you have the children to think of, and besides, the last thing Simon would have wanted was for you to be lonely and miserable for the rest of your life.'

'Who says I'm lonely and miserable?' she protested, but it sounded half-hearted and she knew it, just as she knew that Jenny wouldn't be fooled for one moment into thinking she was happy.

'All I'm saying, Mel,' said Jenny, lightly touching her arm, 'is not to shut yourself away and not to think that you would be betraying Simon in some way if you were to be attracted to someone else.'

'All right, Jen, point taken, but you really are quite wrong where Gareth Morgan is concerned; he certainly isn't interested in me.'

'Well, we shall see,' Jenny replied irritatingly, then added, 'Time will tell. Talking of time——' she glanced at the clock '—I really must be going; the girls will be home from school.'

Much later, when the children were in bed, Melanie sat in front of the television trying to watch the late movie. It was a Kevin Costner film, and he was one of her favourite stars, but for some reason she was finding it difficult to concentrate, and each time his face came on to the screen she found herself reminded of Gareth Morgan. In the end she couldn't make up her mind whether there really was a similarity between the two men or whether Gareth was in her mind because of the conversation she'd had with Jenny.

It really was ridiculous, of course, what Jenny had said. There was not the remotest chance that Gareth could be interested in her, and even if there was she really didn't want to know. She wasn't ready yet to let Simon go, didn't want him to slip away from her and be lost forever, and that, she knew, was what would happen if she started another relationship.

With a sigh she flicked the off button on the remote control. She was probably just tired and that was why her concentration was affected. She decided she would feel much better after a good night's sleep.

Even that eluded her, however, and her sleep was troubled. In her dreams she was searching desperately for Simon but couldn't find him. Her search took her to a stable where an angel with Kevin Costner's face stood guard and, even as she watched, the angel changed into Gareth Morgan.

She awoke with a start and lay staring at the ceiling, her heart thumping wildly.

She stretched out her hand as she had done so many times before and felt the empty space beside her.

It was still very dark, and at last she turned her head and was just able to make out the hands on her bedside clock.

Four o'clock.

With a groan she turned over and buried her face in her pillow.

CHAPTER SIX

'MELANIE, this is Catherine. She comes to visit us quite often.'

'Hello, Catherine.' As Melanie looked down at the lovely dark-eyed child who was helping two of the younger ones to make paper-chains she saw that she had lost all her hair.

The little girl looked up and smiled shyly at Melanie, then transferred her gaze to Gareth. 'Will I be home for Christmas, Gareth?' she asked, the brown eyes huge in the pale heart-shaped face.

'I don't see why not,' Gareth replied firmly, then turned towards the guest-rooms. 'Where's your mum? I haven't seen her yet this time.'

'She's at home with Stephen; he's not well,' Catherine replied seriously, then added, 'Daddy's going to stay with me tonight.'

'That's nice. I'll be along to see you later.'

'Before my treatment?' The little girl looked anxious.

'Yes.' Gareth's tone was reassuring. 'Before your treatment.'

Catherine returned to her paper-chains and Melanie moved down the ward with Gareth.

'She has a very supportive family,' he commented. 'Mum or Dad always stays while she has her treatment, and the other children in the family are kept involved all the time. It's a very sad case; Catherine was found to have a tumour in her abdomen. She's had extensive surgery and is still undergoing chemotherapy. . .' He paused and drew back the curtains around a cot. 'But I guarantee you'll find a different story in here today.'

For one moment Melanie didn't recognise the young girl who looked up at her, her face flushed and smiling, then she realised it was Tracey.

'Baby Daniel had his pyloromyotomy yesterday,' murmured Gareth. 'And he's doing very well, isn't he, Tracey?' He bent over the cot and lightly touched the sleeping baby's cheek with the back of his index finger. Something in the simple gesture moved Melanie, and she was forced to swallow an unexpected lump in her throat.

'Oh, yes, he's fine now,' said Tracey happily. 'He's had some glucose water and Dr Lineham says he can have his first proper feed in a couple of hours' time.'

'Where's Sean?' Melanie glanced round the ward, but couldn't see any sign of the baby's father.

'He's gone to get a couple of Mars bars.' Tracey grinned. 'We suddenly felt hungry—I expect it's because Daniel's eating again, don't you?'

'You're probably right,' said Gareth seriously, then as they moved away, leaving Tracey with her baby, he glanced at Melanie. 'How's Peter?'

'He's much better, thanks.'

'Is he back at school?'

'No, he's at Jenny's today. I thought one more day

at home — just to make sure. . .' She hesitated. 'It was kind of you to bring those stamps, Gareth.' She lowered her voice, aware that Jean was standing at the end of the ward and looked as if she was straining her ears to hear what she and Gareth were saying.

'It was nothing,' he dismissed it. 'I just happened to have them at home — I used to collect them when I was a boy.'

Melanie frowned; it looked as if her sister could have been right in her assumption that stamp-collecting wasn't one of Gareth's interests now.

'I remembered Peter saying he collected stamps,' Gareth went on, unaware of what he had just confirmed, 'and I just thought they might help to cheer him up. . .or at least maybe make him a little more kindly disposed towards me.'

She looked up sharply and was in time to see a rueful smile cross his features. 'What do you mean?' Suddenly she felt uncomfortable.

'Well, let's face it, I wasn't exactly top of Peter's league, was I?'

For one moment she didn't know what to say, because what Gareth had just said was the truth. Peter hadn't liked him, but she could hardly admit that to his face.

She was saved from further embarrassment however as Gareth said, 'Don't worry about it, Melanie. I'm quite used to children, and I would imagine that Peter has become so used to protecting you that he sees any other male as a serious threat.' He glanced up as he spoke, just as Jean began to move purposefully down the ward towards them, the look on her face suggesting she was hell-bent on breaking up any tête-à-tête that was going on. 'Ah, Jean,' he said smoothly, 'come along to the office, will you? There's something I want to discuss with you.'

Melanie wasn't sure whether the look Jean threw her as she went off with Gareth was one of triumph or of dislike. Then she tried to forget the incident as she involved herself with the ward routine.

But as the day went on she found herself constantly recalling what Gareth had said about Peter seeing him as a threat. Was that really what had happened? She hadn't been able to understand her son's apparent dislike of Gareth Morgan, but she hadn't for one moment imagined that could be the reason. She decided she would have to talk to Peter and put the record straight; she couldn't have him worrying unnecessarily.

The rest of the morning on the ward was hectic, and Melanie didn't have another moment to think about Peter, Gareth, or what anyone else might be thinking. But when she went to the canteen to have her lunch, she had no sooner sat down than she was joined by Donna, whom she hadn't yet seen that morning, as Donna had been working on the ward's intensive care unit.

'Good, I've got you on your own!' Donna plonked her tray down and began transferring her lunch to the table.

'I'm sorry?' Melanie stared at her.

'I've been dying to know — we all have — but you've

been off duty and no one quite had the nerve to ask Gareth, but now you can tell me all about it.'

'I don't know what you're talking about.' Melanie frowned, stalling for time, but already she had a sneaking suspicion to what Donna was referring.

'Oh, come on, Melanie.' Donna gave a short laugh. 'You know what I mean. You and Gareth suddenly disappearing like that the other day — where did you go?'

'Where did everyone think we went?' She managed a faint smile at Donna's eager expression.

'No one knew what to think.' Melanie watched as Donna began to tuck enthusiastically into her cottage pie. 'Do you know,' she went on after she'd eaten a couple of mouthfuls, 'in all the time that Gareth's been here, we've never known him to go off early. Everyone's saying you must have something all the others haven't if you can induce him to hand his shift over to someone else.' She set down her knife and fork and stared at Melanie across the table. 'So come on, tell me, how did you manage it?' She leaned forward eagerly, her lunch temporarily forgotten.

'I can assure you, it wasn't anything exciting. . .'

'Let me be the judge of that. . .' Donna's eyes widened knowingly.

'My son was taken ill at his school, that's all.'

'Your son. . .?' echoed Donna disbelievingly.

Melanie nodded. 'Yes, I'm sorry to disappoint you all, but it was no more romantic than that. I tried to ring my sister to ask her to go and fetch him, but I couldn't get hold of her. I don't have any transport of my own, and Gareth kindly offered to drive me to the school to get him.'

'And that's all it was!' Donna looked so disappointed that Melanie was forced to laugh.

'Yes, that's all it was. Honestly. So I'd be obliged, Donna, if you'd tell the others before the gossip gets out of hand.'

'Hmm, I may not tell Jean.' Donna sniffed, then picked up her fork again. 'Let her sweat for a bit.'

'Donna, that's not fair. . .' protested Melanie. 'I don't want Jean under the impression there's something going on between Gareth and me when there isn't.'

'Do her good,' muttered Donna and took another mouthful.

'Donna!'

'Well, it will,' she said, then when she caught sight of Melanie's shocked expression she shrugged and added, 'I get fed up with Jean going on as if she owns Gareth. It's obvious he isn't interested in her. . .'

'He might be for all we know. . .' murmured Melanie.

'Don't be daft. If he was he'd have asked her out by now, wouldn't he?'

'Maybe he has and we don't know about it.'

'Fat chance of that!' Donna exploded. 'You think she'd keep that to herself?'

Melanie shrugged, but smiled in spite of herself, then, growing serious again, she thoughtfully stirred her coffee. 'Even so, I wouldn't want to upset anyone needlessly; there really isn't anything going on between Gareth and me. . . As it is, I've got to convince my son. . .'

'Does he think so as well?' Donna looked up quickly.

'I don't know; it was something Gareth said this morning. He implied that Peter might be protective towards me since. . .since Simon died, and would see any other male as a threat.'

'Do you think that's how he feels?'

'Well, he did seem suspicious of Gareth at first, but I think Gareth won him over in the end. . .' She trailed off as she saw Donna's renewed interest, and wished she hadn't started.

'How? How did he win him over?' Clearly Donna wasn't going to let the matter rest.

'He brought him some stamps for his collection.'

'Really? And when did he do that?' Donna asked, her expression innocent.

'Er — yesterday afternoon. He just popped in to see how Peter was and he brought him the stamps.'

'Oh, just popped in, did he? Of course he knew where to go. I was forgetting, he's been to your house before, hasn't he?'

'Donna, will you please stop looking at me like that?' Melanie pushed her chair back in exasperation and stood up. 'Honestly, what does it take to make you understand that there is absolutely nothing between me and Gareth Morgan?'

'I don't know, Melanie.' Donna grinned. 'But I'll tell you something. Actions speak louder than words, and two visits to your home in one month has to mean something!'

Melanie found that her conversation with Donna had put her on edge. She really wished people would stop jumping to conclusions where she and Gareth were concerned—first her sister, even Peter in a funny sort of way, and now Donna. Why couldn't everyone just mind their own business and let her get on with her life?

Later, when she returned to the ward, she went to sit with Catherine, who had returned from her treatment and was feeling very nauseous.

The curtains were only half drawn round the little girl's bed, and from where she was sitting, through the gap, Melanie could see Gareth talking to a young boy and his parents who had just come on to the ward.

She really didn't know anything about him, she thought idly, watching him while gently she stroked Catherine's forehead. She knew he ran the children's ward calmly and efficiently, but about his life away from the hospital she knew nothing.

He moved out of her line of vision and she found herself leaning forward slightly so that she could still see him. He was as powerfully built as Simon had been slight. He was dark, his hair short, crisp, curling into the nape of his neck. Simon had been fair— blond, even—his eyes grey like Peter's, while Gareth's were dark.

They were so different.

But why was she comparing him with Simon?

Even as she watched, she saw him lean forward and say something to the boy that brought a laughing response. He really was so good with children. He should have children of his own. Maybe he had for all she knew. Maybe he had once loved some woman enough to father her children.

At the thought of that something stirred inside her, some urge she hadn't felt since Simon died, a feeling she'd thought she would never feel again.

Even as she fought to control it, Gareth, as if he sensed her eyes on him, looked up and met her gaze. For a long moment she was unable to look away, and it was as if he could read the thoughts she'd been having.

'Melanie. . .' A little hand touched hers, and quickly she looked down.

'What is it, Catherine?'

'Will you tell me a story?'

'Of course, what would you like?'

'*Peter Pan*.' The little girl pointed to a book on her locker.

'This used to be one of my favourites,' said Melanie as she opened the book. Just before she started reading she glanced across the ward again, but Gareth had moved away from the boy's bed and gone back to his office.

Later that night, after Sophie was in bed and asleep, and during the half-hour that Melanie always tried to devote to Peter, she asked him if he had been bothered by Gareth coming to the house.

'What do you mean?' The suspicious look was back on his face.

'Well, you didn't seem very happy when he brought you home from school, and you did say you didn't like him.'

'I s'pose he's all right.' He shrugged. 'He had some good stamps,' he added as an afterthought.

'Peter. . .' She hesitated, not really sure herself what she was trying to say. 'Gareth is a very kind man and he was only trying to help us out in a difficult situation—but that's all it was.'

'Is he a friend?' asked Peter suspiciously.

'He's not really even that,' she replied carefully. 'He's my boss, that's all.'

'Sophie says he's a friend.'

'Well, Sophie would, but she's a little too young to understand.'

'So he's not your boyfriend?' He looked up at her with his solemn, grey-eyed stare.

'Peter, of course he isn't! Why should you think that?'

'I don't know, really.' He shrugged again. 'I heard Aunty Jen tell Cassie it's about time you had another boyfriend.'

'Oh, she did, did she?' Melanie didn't know whether to laugh or be cross. Leaning forward, she smoothed Peter's hair out of his eyes. 'How would you feel if I did have a boyfriend?' she asked gently.

'I don't know.' He shook his head.

'Would you mind?'

'I s'pose not. . .but. . .it wouldn't be the same, would it?'

'What do you mean?'

He hesitated. 'Well, it wouldn't be Daddy, would it?'

Melanie had to swallow the lump that had risen in her throat. 'No, darling, it wouldn't be Daddy,' she agreed.

'I like it now, just us three,' he said after a while.

'Good, but Peter, you would tell me if there was anything worrying you, wouldn't you?'

He nodded and she bent down to tuck him in and kiss him goodnight, but as she switched out the light he said, 'Mum, will he be coming here again?'

She paused in the open doorway. 'I shouldn't think so, Peter. Why?'

'Oh, nothing. Night, Mum.'

'Goodnight, darling.'

Melanie thought she had put the matter right with Peter and that he wouldn't mention Gareth again, but two days later he came home from school with a look of excitement on his face.

'What is it?' she asked curiously.

'I swapped some stamps at school today and I got a set that Gareth hasn't got. Will you tell him tomorrow, Mum?'

CHAPTER SEVEN

'GARETH, can I have a word, please?' Melanie looked round the office door.

Gareth was sitting at his desk writing a report, and he looked up, his expression softening as he caught sight of her.

'Of course; come in, Melanie.' He indicated for her to shut the door and to take a seat. 'What's the problem?'

'Well, it's not exactly a problem and, to be honest, it isn't to do with work, but I don't seem to have the chance to speak to you at any other time.'

He put down his pen and leaned back in his chair. 'Now you've got me really intrigued.' He grinned, and at the sudden interest in his expression she felt her cheeks grow warm.

'It's Peter, actually,' she carried on quickly in an effort to cover her confusion.

'Peter? He isn't ill again?'

'Oh, no. It's nothing like that. He wanted me to tell you that he swapped some stamps with a boy at school and that he has a set for you that apparently you don't have. I didn't have the heart to tell him that you don't actually collect stamps anymore.'

'I'm glad you didn't!' He stared at her. 'Fancy him thinking of me!'

'Peter's like that.' Suddenly Melanie felt proud.

'Maybe I'm not the ogre I thought I was where Peter's concerned.' He grinned, and Melanie remembered what Jenny had said about his trying to get to her through her children. She shifted uneasily.

'So have you brought them with you?' he asked suddenly.

'What?'

'The stamps?' He raised his eyebrows in amusement.

Feeling silly, and wishing he would stop looking at her in that way, she shook her head. 'No, I got the impression Peter wants to give them to you himself.'

He smiled then, his eyes crinkling again at the corners. 'I see,' he said slowly. 'Well, in that case, I'd better come and see him. That is,' he added softly, 'if that's all right with his mum.'

'Well, yes, of course.' She felt her cheeks growing even hotter. 'When would you like to come?'

'When would you like me to come?'

She had the feeling he was playing games with her. 'How about this evening?' She tried to sound casual, matter-of-fact. 'Would that be convenient?'

'This evening it is. I shall look forward to it.' He stood up and walked round the desk.

'I must get on,' she murmured as she too stood up and turned towards the door. 'There's an emergency asthmatic on the way in. . .' She reached out for the door-handle at the same moment as him. His hand covered hers. His touch, warm and unexpected, was a shock.

She remained very still, expecting him to withdraw his hand immediately, and when he didn't she eventually raised her eyes to meet his.

He was standing very close to her, so close that she caught that woody tang of his aftershave, but this time underneath that was another, deeper scent — the maleness, the very essence of the man.

'Melanie. . . I . . .' he began, and she held her breath, but it seemed she was not to know what he had been about to say, because at that moment someone tapped on the door and turned the handle. They both jumped and drew their hands back as the door opened and they found themselves face to face with Jean.

She stared suspiciously from Melanie to Gareth, then back to Melanie again. 'I was looking for you,' she said, her tone accusing. 'There's an emergency admission on its way in.'

'Yes, I know; I'm on my way.' Without another glance at either Gareth or Jean, Melanie hurried on to the ward.

The moment had disturbed her — Jean's accusing look, as if she and Gareth had been up to something . . .but, much more than that, his closeness and the warmth of his hand on hers had caused her pulse to race. Desperately she tried to pull herself together. What in the world was wrong with her? She was acting like a silly schoolgirl instead of a mature woman with two children.

Resolutely she lifted her chin and, smoothing down her dinosaur apron, she went to meet the new arrival.

But the thought that remained firmly at the back of her mind and would not go, no matter how hard she tried, was that Gareth would be coming to the house that night.

The asthmatic was an eleven-year-old boy called Scott Flynn who had been taken ill in the gym at his school and was accompanied by his housemaster, a Mr Prowse.

Melanie immediately set up a nebuliser to assist Scott's breathing, then when the boy was a little more comfortable she attempted to take some admission details from the teacher.

'Have his parents been informed?' she asked.

'The headmaster was trying to contact them,' replied Mr Prowse, 'but Scott's father is a company rep and is on the road somewhere, and his mother was not at home. I'm sure the headmaster will keep trying.'

'Is Scott prone to asthma attacks at school?'

'He hasn't had one for a long time, although we were aware of the fact that he suffered from asthma.' Mr Prowse sounded worried. 'He always carried a Ventolin inhaler with him, but today it didn't have much effect. He will be all right, won't he, nurse?' Turning aside so that the boy wouldn't hear, he murmured, 'He looked dreadful in the ambulance; he was really fighting for his breath—I thought he was going to die.'

'His breathing is getting easier now,' said Melanie reassuringly. 'Have you any idea what triggered the attack?'

'Well, the boys were rope-climbing, and Scott wanted to have a go. As I said, it's been so long since he had an attack that I'd almost forgotten about his asthma. Anyway, I let him. He seemed to be all right until he got to the top of the rope, then he said he was stuck. I tried to talk him down, but I suppose he panicked and the stress brought on the attack. By the time we got him down he was wheezing badly. Oh, God, I hope he's going to be OK; what would I tell his parents. . .?'

'Try not to worry,' replied Melanie. 'I'm sure everything will be all right now that he's here and we have things under control. Shall I see if I can get you a cup of tea? You look as if you could do with one.'

'That's very kind of you, Nurse, thank you.' Mr Prowse ran his fingers through his hair in a frantic gesture.

Dr Lineham arrived at that moment to examine Scott, and Melanie asked the teacher to sit in the visitors' waiting-room while she went to the kitchen.

Her heart sank when she found Jean in the room, and she hoped she could get out again without getting into conversation with her, but Jean obviously had other ideas, for as Melanie turned to leave she barred her way.

'In future, Melanie,' she said icily, 'if you have any sort of problem would you please come to me and not bother Charge Nurse Morgan with it? He has more than enough to do as it is, and as I'm acting sister on this ward I'm perfectly capable of dealing with any problems that arise.'

'I'm sure you are,' replied Melanie calmly, 'but the reason I went to Gareth had nothing to do with the ward.'

'What do you mean?' Jean frowned. 'What was it about, then?'

Melanie took a deep breath. She hadn't wanted to tell Jean, but the other woman hadn't really left her any alternative. 'It was a personal matter.'

As she saw Jean's expression change she realised she'd only made matters worse. 'To do with my son,' she added quickly, before Jean could misinterpret the facts even further.

'Your son? Honestly, Melanie——' Jean's lip curled '—you must learn to leave your personal problems at home. This is just the type of thing Gareth doesn't want to be bothered with. We've had more than enough of that sort of thing in the past. So what was the problem? I suppose you were wanting time off.'

'No, Jean,' she replied steadily, holding on to her temper with difficulty, 'it was nothing like that.'

'Then what?' the other woman demanded.

'It was as I said.' Melanie stuck to her guns. 'A personal matter and nothing to do with anyone else.'

An angry expression flitted across Jean's features, but before she had time to comment further there came sounds of a commotion on the ward.

'What the devil's happening?' Jean stared at Melanie, then they both left what they were doing and hurried outside.

'Where is he? Where's my son?' A distraught

woman was rushing through the ward, peering into cubicles and whisking back curtains. 'Scott! Scott! Where are you?'

Other children on the ward were beginning to cry, alarmed and frightened by what was happening.

Gareth came out of his office and moved swiftly down the ward towards the woman. 'Mrs Flynn? Would you like to come with me?' He took hold of her arm.

Angrily she spun round and stared up at him. 'Where is he? What's happened to him? I knew this would happen. I told them he wasn't to do games, but would they listen?' Her eyes were wild, her dark hair dishevelled.

Melanie felt sorry for her, knowing how she would have felt if it had been Peter.

Just as Gareth appeared to have calmed the woman slightly and was leading her down the ward towards the cubicle where they had put Scott, Mr Prowse suddenly stepped out of the room where he had been waiting and Mrs Flynn caught sight of him.

'Oh, it's you!' she shouted, and Mr Prowse visibly paled. 'I might have guessed it would be you.' She turned to Gareth. 'All he thinks about is games and gym,' she yelled angrily, then, turning back to the unfortunate teacher, she pointed her finger at him and added, 'Well, I tell you now, if anything has happened to Scott, I'll hold you personally responsible.'

'Mrs Flynn, please calm down. Nothing has happened to Scott,' said Gareth gently. 'Look, see for yourself.' He pulled back the curtains around Scott's bed.

Dr Lineham had just taken the boy off the nebuliser, and he was sitting on the side of the bed. He stared at his mother in embarrassment. 'Mum! For goodness' sake!' Furtively he glanced round at the other children in the ward. 'Don't make such a fuss — I'm perfectly all right!'

One of the children began to giggle, quickly followed by another. Dr Lineham beckoned Mrs Flynn into the cubicle, winked at Gareth, and drew the curtains again.

'Right ——' Gareth looked round the ward '— the excitement's over.' He crossed to the far end of the ward, switched on the radio, and allowed the familiar voice of Simon Bates to restore normality to the ward.

'Phew!' Mr Prowse sank down on the nearest chair, his face white.

'I would say you need that cup of tea more than ever,' said Melanie. 'I'll get it for you; it's already made — I just came out to see what all the noise was about.'

Fortunately, in all the furore it seemed that Jean had become side-tracked. When Melanie returned with the tea she saw that she was with Catherine, who had been fretful all day, and later, when all the excitement had died down, Melanie found to her relief that Jean had gone off duty.

'What time's he coming?' Peter stared at her across the table.

'I don't know exactly,' she admitted. 'He just said this evening.'

'I'm not going to bed until he'th been,' announced Sophie flatly.

'Well, we'll have to see how late it gets,' replied Melanie dubiously. It was quite obvious her daughter was delighted at the prospect of seeing Gareth again, and even Peter seemed pleased, if more guardedly so.

What Melanie was reluctant to admit, however, even to herself, was how much she was looking forward to the visit.

And an hour later, after Sophie had had her bath and was in her Disney nightshirt, and the doorbell finally rang, she found her heart beating rapidly as her daughter rushed to open the front door.

She remained in the lounge with Peter, and after an intriguing silence from the hall they heard Sophie's squeal of delight before she burst back into the room, wearing a baseball cap. Melanie was amused to see that Gareth had even pulled Sophie's hair through the gap at the back of the cap.

As he followed the little girl into the lounge his eyes immediately met Melanie's. 'Hello, hope I'm not too late.' He gave an apologetic grin.

'No, of course not,' she murmured.

'Hello.' He turned to Peter, who had just switched off the television. 'Your mum tells me you wanted to see me.'

Peter nodded importantly and, crossing the room, took an envelope from behind the clock.

'A boy at school had that set of Canadian stamps you said you didn't have, so I did a swap for you.'

'That was really good of you, Peter. Thank you.' Gareth leaned eagerly over the table as Peter shook out the stamps, and for the next ten minutes they retreated into a world of their own.

Sophie was barely able to contain her impatience, and in the end Melanie sent her off to feed her rabbit while she sat quietly watching as Peter and Gareth solemnly concluded their business.

'I'm not sure how I can repay you for this,' she heard Gareth say.

'That's all right,' replied Peter gruffly, 'You gave me all those other stamps.'

'Even so. . .' Gareth hesitated. '. . .I would still like to do something.' He glanced at Melanie, then back to Peter. 'Do you like fishing?' he asked.

'I don't know; I've never been,' Peter admitted.

'Never been?' Gareth sounded amazed. 'Well, we must do something about that. I go fairly often; maybe your mum would let you come with me one day.'

'Mum. . .?' Peter sounded a bit doubtful, but Melanie noticed a gleam in his eyes as he quickly turned to look at her.

'That's very kind of Gareth; we'll have to see what we can arrange. . .' she began, then turned sharply as Sophie came into the lounge, carrying Bengie. 'Sophie——' she sighed '—how many more times do I have to tell you? Please don't bring Bengie in here.'

'I want to pretend he'th a dog,' protested Sophie.

'I know, but he's not a dog, he's a rabbit, so please take him back to his hutch.'

'Want a dog. Not fair,' muttered Sophie.

Melanie shot Gareth a helpless look. 'She's been on about a dog for months.'

'And you're not keen on the idea?' he asked.

'It isn't that. I love dogs; it's just that I don't think it would be fair as we're out all day.'

'And what about you, Peter? Would you like a dog as well?'

Peter nodded. 'Yes, but I wouldn't like it to be on its own all day.'

The next minute Sophie appeared again, this time dragging a large box behind her.

'Oh, Sophie, no,' Melanie protested. 'Gareth doesn't want to see our tatty old Christmas decorations. We're trying to make do,' she explained, 'without buying any new ones; they are all so expensive in the shops.' Turning back to her daughter, she said, 'Come on, Sophie, take those back to the cupboard and then it'll be time for bed.'

'Oh, no!' wailed Sophie. 'I want to thtay with Gareth.'

By some unspoken agreement Gareth stayed until Melanie had got the children to bed. When she came back into the lounge she found him studying the framed photograph that stood on the television of herself with Simon and the children, taken soon after Sophie was born.

For one moment she thought Gareth was going to

say something about Simon; instead he turned and looked at her, the photograph in his hand. 'You had your hair short then,' he observed.

She smiled. 'Yes.'

'I like it better long — the way you wear it now.' His gaze roamed over her hair which, when she was off duty, she wore loose.

Quickly she looked away, suddenly afraid at what might be in his eyes, uncertain that she could cope.

A long, awkward silence followed, during which she desperately sought for something to say. Then deliberately Gareth replaced the photograph on the mantelpiece and turned towards her.

'Sorry Sophie is so precocious,' she said frantically. 'I think it must be because she misses her father so much. . . Anyway, she's in bed now. . .' She pulled a face at a sudden thump from above. 'At least, I hope she's in bed! Peter seemed quite tired, but he was really pleased you asked him to go fishing; he's never been fishing before——'

'Melanie——' he intervened gently.

'Of course,' she went on, knowing she was waffling but determined to keep the conversation going — anything to prevent what she thought might be about to happen. 'I'm not into fishing and I don't think even Sophie would be, in spite of her being such a tomboy——'

'Melanie!'

'Yes?' Helplessly she looked up at him.

'That's better,' he said softly after the silence that

followed. 'I can't tell you what I want to say if you don't stop talking.'

She gave a helpless little gesture, but remained silent, suddenly keenly aware of him once more — of his size, his sheer masculinity and of how fragile and feminine he made her feel.

'You must be aware of what I'm starting to feel about you,' he said softly. When she didn't reply he put his hands on her shoulders and stood for a long moment looking down at her. Then with one hand he tilted her chin so that she was forced to look up at him. The hint of amusement was still in the dark eyes, but there was also a tenderness she hadn't seen before.

'I think I was beginning to get the message,' she murmured at last.

'And how do you feel about it?'

'I don't know, Gareth.' She shook her head. 'I'm really not sure,' she added helplessly.

'Would you come out with me some time so that we can get to know each other better? We hardly have the chance for that on the ward.'

'That's true,' she agreed, thinking of the gossip that would be sure to follow if they were to publicly advance their friendship.

'So what do you say, then? Will you come out with me one night?' There was eagerness now in his voice. 'How about at the weekend? Would your sister have the children? Maybe we could go to that new restaurant in town. . .'

Suddenly it all seemed to Melanie to be moving too fast, and abruptly she pulled away from him. 'I don't know, Gareth,' she said sharply. 'I'm sorry, I really don't know. . . I'm not sure that I can. . . It's too soon, you see.'

Instinctively they both looked at the photograph of Simon.

Then as they turned to each other again she gave a deep sigh. 'I'm sorry, Gareth, really I am. I don't expect you to understand.'

'Maybe I understand much better than you think,' he said softly.

She shook her head. 'No, it's impossible for anyone to understand fully unless they've been in this situation,' she said firmly. 'I used to think I understood how someone felt who had been bereaved, but I didn't, not really. . .' She trailed off as her eyes filled with sudden tears.

'Don't you think it's about time you told me about Simon?' he asked quietly.

'You mean you really want to know?'

'Of course I do. Did you think I wouldn't?' He seemed puzzled.

'I don't know.' She shrugged and turned away. 'I find more and more these days I avoid talking about him; I suppose I think people will either get bored with hearing the same things or will think me morbid.'

'Well, I won't.' He sat down on the settee and held out his hand indicating for her to join him. 'You won't bore me because I haven't heard any of it before, but, apart from that, I happen to think the more you talk about it, the sooner you'll start to come to terms with it.'

Carefully avoiding his outstretched hand, she took her place beside him, not as close as he had obviously intended, but close enough.

'So what do you want to know? Where shall I start?'

'How about at the beginning? I can just hear Sophie saying that would be a very good place to start.'

They both laughed then, and it lightened the tension that had grown between them.

'All right,' she agreed at last. 'At the beginning it shall be.' She paused reflectively. 'Simon and I met at school,' she began at last.

'Childhood sweethearts?'

She nodded. 'Yes, I suppose you could say that. We dated for a couple of years, then I went away to do my nursing training.'

'And Simon?'

'He went into the police force.' She was silent for a moment, remembering. 'Everyone thought we would split up, being separated,' she went on, 'but it only seemed to strengthen our relationship. We travelled to see each other as often as we could when we were off duty. We got engaged on my twenty-first birthday, my parents gave a party. . .and we were married a year later.' She swallowed. The only sound in the room was the ticking of the clock. Gareth remained very still and silent beside her, waiting for her to go on.

'It was a big white wedding at our local church with a hotel reception — everything I had ever dreamed of . . .only it wasn't to last.' She paused. 'Peter was born a year later. . .and then Sophie. . . We were so happy. . .' The smile faded and she trailed off and sat staring at her hands.

'What happened, Melanie?'

She looked up sharply as Gareth spoke; she'd become so lost in her thoughts that she'd almost forgotten he was there.

'Happened. . .?' She frowned.

'Yes, to Simon,' he said gently. 'Was he ill?'

'No.' She shook her head, then gave a faint smile. 'Simon never had a day's illness in his life — that's the ironic part.'

'Then what. . .?' He frowned.

'He was killed.'

'A road accident?'

She shook her head again, then took a deep breath. 'No, Simon was murdered. He was shot.'

She became aware that Gareth was staring at her with a look of amazed horror, a look which she had become familiar with whenever she told anyone the circumstances of her husband's death.

'It was during a bank raid,' she went on. 'An armed gang. Simon went to the aid of an elderly woman customer in the bank who appeared to be having a heart attack. One of the gang yelled at him, warned him not to go any closer, but Simon ignored him, so he shot him — it was as simple as that. One moment he was alive, intent on helping someone, the next he was dead. . .' She trailed off as the words became stuck in her throat, and her gaze met Gareth's.

'My God, Melanie.' His voice was shaky, charged with emotion. 'You poor little thing.' Without another word he opened his arms and enfolded her, drawing her close.

It felt warm and safe in the circle of his arms, and with a sound that could easily have been a sob she rested her head against his chest.

CHAPTER EIGHT

FOR a long time Gareth simply held Melanie, and gradually she felt calmed and comforted by the steady beating of his heart. Then at last, when she stirred, he gently held her away from him and looked at her.

'I'm so sorry, Melanie,' he said. 'I had no idea — none of us on the ward did. Why didn't you tell us when you first came?'

'I wanted to make a completely fresh start — there was so much publicity about it where I came from. The children were so aware of it, and I felt I owed it to them to try and put it all behind us.'

'You owe it to yourself as well,' he said softly.

'I know.' She swallowed and looked away.

He was very still for a moment, then once again he reached out his hand and gently touched her cheek, and with his thumb beneath her chin tilted her face towards him.

'It will get easier, you know, in time.' His voice was very low. 'Will you let me help it become easier for you?'

Melanie found herself staring at his mouth and wondering what it would be like to be kissed by him. Already she was surprised by how good it felt to be held by a man again. . . It had been so long.

Still mesmerised by the finely shaped curve of his lips, she remained perfectly still as he moved closer.

It came as no surprise when his mouth touched hers. It was the gentlest of kisses, soft and so very tender for such a large, masculine man.

Still she didn't move, content to be the receiver, but at the same time surprised to find how much she enjoyed it.

Maybe because she offered no resistance he grew bolder, increasing the pressure of his mouth, gently persuading her lips to part while he cradled her face in both his hands, his fingers entangled in her hair.

Deep inside she felt the stirring of some longing, some passion she had almost forgotten, a yearning she'd thought had died with Simon.

Gareth must have detected her sudden surge of desire, and his own passion flared to match hers. For a moment the soft, gentle man disappeared and the full-blooded, passionate nature of the man beneath was revealed as with hands and tongue he aroused and excited her.

It had been so long since she had felt like this. . . Sex had always been so good. . . The old feelings were still there. . .lying dormant. . .just waiting to be aroused.

Simon had always known how to turn her on. . . but this wasn't Simon, this was Gareth, and he was very different from Simon. . .

Abruptly she pulled away, pressing the back of her hand to her mouth. 'I'm sorry, Gareth. . . I can't. . . not yet. . . It's too soon; I'm simply not ready.'

For a moment he looked shaken, as if the kiss they

had shared had affected him too and he was forced to fight for control.

'I'm sorry,' she said again, her voice little more than a whisper.

Still breathing deeply, he stared at her for a long moment. 'All right,' he said at last, his voice quiet and controlled now. 'So we take it slowly. I'm not in any hurry; I'm not going anywhere. I won't rush you.'

'But that wouldn't be fair to you, Gareth.' She frowned, then added, 'You see, what I'm trying to say is that I'm not sure I want to even date anyone yet.'

'That's OK; that's what I thought you meant. As I said, there's no hurry. We have all the time in the world, and if you don't feel ready to start dating I suggest we be friends and just see what happens. If I'm honest, I'm a bit wary of long-term commitments myself,' he went on, then added, 'But we are friends, aren't we, Melanie?'

'Of course, but——'

'No buts. . . We won't go out alone if you don't want to. Suppose we simply take the children out?'

'The children. . .?' her eyes widened.

'How about taking them somewhere for the day on Sunday?'

'What did you have in mind?' she asked, wondering what Peter's reaction would be.

'Well, I have a match in the afternoon—maybe Sophie would like to see that.' He grinned, his face suddenly lighting up as the seriousness of the mood vanished. 'But I could pick you up in the morning and we could go somewhere first, then maybe have lunch. . . Do you think they would like that?'

'I'm sure they would,' Melanie replied slowly.

'And how about you? Would you like that?'

She was silent for a moment, considering, and he, misinterpreting her silence, lifted his hand and very gently ran the back of his fingers down her cheek.

She jumped and raised startled eyes to his.

'Melanie, I promise that is all it will be — no strings attached, simply a day out with the children.'

'All right, Gareth,' she replied at last. 'I would like that. . . I'm sorry to be like this, I really am; you must think me an awful wimp. . .'

'I don't think anything of the sort. I quite understand how you feel, and you have my word I won't put you under any pressure.' He drew away from her then and stood up. 'And now,' he said firmly, 'I really must be going. I'll see you in the morning, bright and early.'

'Of course, and thank you, Gareth.' She smiled and he stood for a long moment looking down at her, then with a final glance at the photograph on the television he moved towards the door.

'We'll make arrangements for Sunday later in the week,' he said, then as he stepped into the hall he added, 'Maybe you'd better tell the children; they may not want to go.'

'I don't think there'll be any danger of that.' Melanie smiled. 'There haven't been too many outings recently.' She opened the front door and he stepped outside, then paused and looked back at her.

'Even so, there could still be a certain amount of wariness, especially from Peter.'

'Not Sophie?' She raised her eyebrows with a laugh.

'No, not Sophie,' he replied drily.

He went then, strolling in his unhurried way down the path to his jeep. Starting the engine, he reversed, turned the vehicle round, then with a wave of his hand he was gone.

Melanie stood for a moment in the open doorway, then quietly closed the front door. She had imagined that when she had rebuffed him after he had kissed her he would not be bothered with her any more. But it seemed as if she was wrong. It looked as if he really was prepared to settle for friendship, and if that was the case she felt she could cope. Friendship she was ready for; passion was something else all together. Passion belonged to Simon and to the past they had shared, a past she was not yet ready to let go.

She was about to go back into the lounge when a slight movement from upstairs caught her eye. Looking up, she saw Peter and Sophie kneeling on the landing, their faces pressed between the rails of the banisters.

'What are you two doing?' She laughed. 'I thought you would both be asleep by now!'

'What did Gareth mean — we may not want to go?' asked Peter suspiciously.

'Go where?' demanded Sophie.

Melanie sighed and began to climb the stairs. 'I was going to tell you in the morning,' she protested. 'Gareth is going to take us out on Sunday.'

'All of us?' There was still a note of doubt in Peter's voice.

'Where?' demanded Sophie, scrambling to her feet.

'Yes, all of us.' Melanie looked down at Peter, who was still kneeling by the rails, then, turning to Sophie, she added, I don't know where; he didn't say.'

'Can I wear my batheball cap?'

'Will we go in the jeep?' asked Peter.

'I don't know; I expect so,' said Melanie, then, as Sophie began hopping up and down in excitement, and even Peter's eyes lit up,' she said, 'But nobody will be going anywhere if you don't get yourselves to bed. At this rate you won't be up for school tomorrow.'

At last she got them settled, and when the house was quiet she went downstairs and into the lounge. Slowly she walked across the room and, picking up Simon's photograph, she stared at it for a long time, then with a deep sigh she replaced it on the television, switched out the light and, closing the door behind her, went up the stairs to bed. She knew she had made the right decision in not becoming too involved with Gareth, knew she was being sensible.

But in spite of that her last thought before falling asleep was of the moment that Gareth had kissed her, the warmth of his body, the pressure of his hands and the stirring of passion inside herself that she thought had died forever.

Melanie stood in the nurses' room and stared at the on-duty rota for the Christmas period. As she ran her finger down the list she saw to her dismay that she was down to work on the afternoon of the children's Nativity play. Her first reaction was that she would have to ask if she could change duties with one of the other nurses.

'If there are problems with the Christmas rota you are to sort them out with me and not bother Gareth.'

Melanie swung round and saw that Jean and two other nurses had come into the room.

Jean was staring at Melanie almost as if she could read what she had been thinking. 'Gareth worked out the list, but he's asked me to take responsibility for the off-duty from now on,' she added, a smug expression on her face.

'Rather you than me,' one of the other nurses replied with a laugh. 'But if you will take on acting sister it's what you must expect.'

Melanie bit her lip. Jean was the last person she wanted to approach about this, but if she went to Gareth now it would look as if she was deliberately flouting Jean's authority and going over her head.

'I take it you don't have any problems, Melanie?' There was already a slightly sarcastic note in Jean's voice. 'It looks as if Gareth has already been pretty lenient with you over the Christmas period as it is.'

'And that's how it should be.' Donna had come up behind them and intervened. 'Melanie has kids; it's only right she should be with them, especially on Christmas Day. There are plenty of us who don't have any kids, to cover for those who do.'

'Well, let's just hope she appreciates it.'

'Actually, Jean——' Melanie took a deep breath '—I am very pleased to have Christmas Day off, but I do have a bit of a problem on the twentieth of December. I see I'm down for a late shift, and I really do need the afternoon off.'

'Well, that's out of the question.' Jean squinted at the board. 'Gareth's off that day, Marlene is going away, Julie is on leave, and it's my day off. I'll swap Christmas Day with you, if you like,' she added spitefully.

Melanie remained silent, and Donna threw her a quick look. 'Was it something important, Melanie?'

She nodded. 'Yes, it was actually. The children are both in a school Nativity play.'

'Oh, but you must go to that! For God's sake, Jean, surely we can work something out?' Donna glared indignantly.

'I don't see how.' Jean shrugged. 'If I start showing preferential treatment for one, everyone will want to change. The next thing you know, people will want time off for Christmas shopping!'

'So?' Donna was clearly getting annoyed, and Melanie put a restraining hand on her arm.

'It's OK, Donna,' she murmured.

'No, it isn't OK,' Donna replied heatedly. 'And I'm sure if Gareth knew the circumstances he would arrange something——'

'Gareth is not to be bothered with these silly things,' snapped Jean. 'I've told you before, he has far more to do than worry about our petty differences.' She stalked off on to the ward, leaving Melanie and Donna alone.

'She really is the limit.' Donna gave an exasperated sigh. 'Ever since Gareth gave her more responsibility on the ward it's gone to her head. You'd have every right to go to Gareth over this, you know, Melanie.'

'I don't want to cause trouble.'

'I know, but you can't let your kids down, can you?'

Helplessly Melanie shook her head.

'The stupid part is if Gareth knew he'd do something about it. He's really good over things like that.' Donna paused, then smiled. 'And especially if he knew it was you.'

Melanie felt her cheeks grow red. 'What's that supposed to mean?'

'You know very well. He's shown an interest in you right from the start, and that's what Jean can't stand. She only said yesterday that she reckons you're after Gareth.'

'She said that?' Melanie's eyes widened in dismay.

Donna nodded, then grinned. 'Looks like she's going to step up her campaign—should be interesting to see who wins.'

'Donna——' Melanie took a deep breath '—I'd be obliged if you would tell Jean, and anyone else you think it may apply to, that I'm not "after" Gareth Morgan, as you put it. I'm not after anyone, and I'm sick and tired of everyone jumping to conclusions.'

'But——'

'I don't want anyone else. Just because I'm a

widow, everyone seems to think I'm easy game. I loved my husband very much. . .and I'm not ready for another relationship, ' she choked. 'I just wish everyone would leave me alone and let me get on with my own life.'

'I say, Melanie, I'm sorry; I didn't know. . .' Donna tried to detain her, but Melanie rushed from the nurses' room, her eyes blinded by sudden angry tears.

She locked herself in the loo and splashed her face with cold water, and ten minutes later, when she presented herself on the ward, she felt more composed. She needn't have worried, however, that anyone would notice, because apart from Donna, who threw her an anxious glance, everyone else was up to their eyes in work.

There was the usual routine Theatre list that morning with tonsillectomies, a hernia and an appendicectomy. There were several children at the 'nearly better' stage who demanded much attention, and Catherine, who was not making the progress they had hoped for. As Melanie passed her bed the little girl called her over.

'Will I be able to go home today, Melanie?' she asked.

'I don't think today, Catherine,' Melanie replied, 'but maybe soon.'

'Gareth said I would be home for Christmas. . .'

'Are you looking forward to Christmas?'

'Yes.' Catherine nodded. 'I'm going carol-singing with my sister.'

'That's lovely. I used to go carol-singing when I was a little girl,' said Melanie, then asked, 'Is your school doing a Nativity play, Catherine?'

'Yes, I was going to be an angel, but I can't now, because I'm in here.' Her eyes clouded over.

Melanie felt a stab of pity for the little girl as she remembered how excited Sophie was over her part in her school's Nativity.

'Tell you what——' she stared thoughtfully at Catherine '—would you like to make a model stable with the crib and the shepherds and everything?'

'How?' Catherine looked dubious.

'Well, I'll try and find as many bits and pieces as I can for you in my lunch break so that you can make a start, and then anything else you need I'll bring from home. How about that?'

Catherine's eyes began to shine, then Melanie glanced up and saw Jean staring at her from the end of the ward.

'I have to go now, Catherine, but you read your book and I'll be back later.' She hurried on down the ward to get another of the children ready for Theatre, and was just remaking the bed when she saw Gareth making his way towards her. She felt her heart leap as his eyes met hers and he smiled.

'Hello,' he said softly. 'Everything all right?'

'Yes.' She longed to tell him about the duty rota, certain he would understand, but she didn't quite dare, knowing the trouble it would cause on the ward.

'Have you told the children about Sunday?'

For one moment she thought she detected a trace

of anxiety in his voice, then when she saw the touch of amusement in his eyes thought she must have been mistaken.

'I have.'

'And what was the reaction?'

'They were delighted.'

'Even Peter?'

'Even Peter,' she replied firmly. 'They're really looking forward to it.'

'And their mum? Is she looking forward to it as well?' A smile hovered around his mouth.

'Yes,' she said, 'their mum's looking forward to it as well. She doesn't get too many outings these days; it will make a nice change.'

'Good; now I suppose I'd better get on with what I came to tell you, hadn't I, Staff Nurse Darby?'

'Yes, Charge Nurse Morgan, I think you had,' she replied solemnly.

'I'd like you to come into the office for a case conference when you've finished what you're doing.'

'I've finished now.' She followed him down the ward, suddenly very aware of him again, and knowing instinctively that he too was thinking of the previous evening.

Jean was already in the office, together with the other members of staff to be included in the case conference. She looked up as Melanie entered the room, and Melanie found herself wondering what Jean would say if she knew what had happened the night before.

She shivered, and Donna glanced at her. 'Are you OK now?' She sounded anxious.

'Yes, I'm fine. Someone just walked over my grave, as my grandmother used to say.'

Further conversation was curtailed then as Dr Lineham arrived and Gareth started the case conference.

'We have a child coming in after lunch,' he began, 'a six-year-old boy for investigations. He has a history of chronic constipation. Apparently his mother is unable to stay with him, so I'd like one of you to take him under your wing.' He glanced round as he spoke, his gaze coming to rest on Melanie.

'Do we know why the mother can't stay?' asked Susan Lineham.

'There are two other children at home,' replied Gareth, 'but there are other circumstances with this case which you need to know about.'

He paused and looked round at his staff before continuing. 'Apparently,' he continued when he saw he had their undivided attention, 'the father left home just over a year ago to live with his girlfriend. Mother was devastated at first, then became very strict with the children. That however now seems to have changed and she doesn't seem bothered about them. Andrew's condition was first noticed by his teacher when he started to soil his pants at school, and the school medical team became involved. It then came out that he wets the bed most nights, but that in spite of soiling his pants he suffers from chronic constipation.'

As Gareth finished speaking, a silence followed, then Donna looked up. 'Do you think we could be looking at a case of abuse?' she asked quietly, voicing the question that everyone else was thinking.

'Maybe,' said Gareth, 'or possibly neglect. Whatever it is, we could have a very distressed, frightened little boy on our hands. Melanie, I would like you to do his admission and look after him.'

Gareth glanced in Melanie's direction, and Jean's head jerked up. 'Melanie's involved with the children for Theatre this morning,' she said quickly. 'I'll see to this child, Gareth.'

'No, that's all right, Jean,' Gareth replied smoothly. 'He's not coming until after lunch; the theatre list will be over by then, and besides, you have your hands full with Catherine at the moment.'

Gareth went on then to discuss further details of Catherine's treatment and the care plans for two other children. But as they all filed back on to the ward, Melanie caught sight of Jean's expression, and she knew that Gareth's choosing her to look after the new patient had given Jean even more cause to believe there was something going on between herself and the charge nurse.

CHAPTER NINE

MELANIE spent most of her lunch break collecting pieces of cardboard and coloured paper for Catherine to start her model of the Nativity.

The little girl's eyes lit up as Melanie placed the items on her bed.

'I've drawn the shapes of the figures on the cardboard,' she explained, 'so maybe this afternoon you could start cutting them out. We could stick different coloured paper on to them for their clothes, then we could secure them on to the base with plasticine so that they will stand up.'

'I'd like them to have real clothes,' said Catherine wistfully.

'I don't think we have much in the way of scraps of material in here,' said Melanie, looking round. 'But I tell you what, I have a rummage bag at home. I'll have a look in there tonight and see what I can find.'

'What's a rummage bag?'

'It's a huge bag full of bits and pieces from everything I've ever made—I expect your mummy has one as well.'

Catherine shook her head. 'My mummy doesn't have time to make things; she goes out to work.'

'I know the feeling; I don't have much time now,' said Melanie ruefully, 'but when my children were small I used to make all their clothes. My little girl loves looking through my rummage bag.'

'What's your little girl's name?' Catherine looked curiously at her, as if she found it hard to believe that nurses should have children.

'Sophie.'

'Is she in a Nativity play?'

Melanie hesitated, but only for a moment. 'Yes, Catherine, she is,' she replied.

'Is she an angel?' The wistful note was back.

'No, she didn't want to be an angel. She's an ass.'

'You mean like a donkey?' Catherine's eyes widened.

'Yes, like a donkey—that's exactly what Sophie wanted to be, so that she could wear a mask.'

Catherine giggled. 'Will you cut out the shape of an ass for my Nativity?'

'Well, I'll have a go——' she glanced up as she spoke '—but it'll have to be later, because I have to go and see a little boy now who has just arrived.'

'What's his name?'

'Andrew.'

'Will he come and talk to me?'

'I'm sure he will.'

She found Andrew in the office with his mother, his sister Joanne and Gareth.

'Ah, here comes your special nurse, Andrew,' Gareth looked up, and as his eyes met hers she had the sudden ridiculous feeling that he was about to say that she was his special nurse as well. 'Her name is

Melanie, and she will be looking after you,' he went on, and the moment was gone. 'Melanie, I would like you to meet Andrew and his family.'

'Hello, Andrew.' Melanie smiled down at the small boy, who was trying to hide behind his mother.

'For Christ's sake, Andrew, stop being so stupid.' His mother pushed him forward. 'Sorry. . .' She rolled her eyes, then realised that her daughter was scribbling on a folder on the desk. 'What the hell d'you think you're doing, Joanne? Leave that alone!'

'It's quite all right,' said Gareth quietly. 'It's an empty folder.'

'That's not the point — she's got to learn to behave.'

'Tell you what, suppose I take Joanne to the playroom while you and Andrew talk to Melanie?' suggested Gareth.

Andrew cowered even further behind his mother, but Joanne went off quite happily with Gareth.

Melanie sat down, opened a folder that had Andrew's name on the front, and began to fill in his admission forms. After she had completed details of his age and address, she turned to his mother, whose name turned out to be Shirley, and said, 'Can you tell me when you first noticed that Andrew was constipated?'

'No.' The woman shrugged. 'How would I know? He doesn't tell me everything.'

'Does he go to the toilet every morning after his breakfast?'

'We don't usually have breakfast — no time in the mornings.'

'So doesn't Andrew have anything to eat before he goes to school?'

'I have a packet of crisps.' It was the first thing the little boy had said.

'And where do you eat your crisps, Andrew?' asked Melanie gently.

'On the way to school.' His gaze flickered to his mother, and she nodded as if to confirm what he had said.

'When was Andrew completely toilet-trained?' Melanie, trying hard to fight her growing irritation, turned her attention back to the woman sitting opposite.

'Oh, I don't know; I can't remember things like that. . .'

'Could you try and remember. . .? The doctor will need to know.'

'Well, let me think about it,' said Shirley. 'He was late, I know that; he always was a dirty little tyke. I remember telling someone once I thought he'd be in nappies when he went to school.'

'And was he?' Melanie asked quietly.

'No, he was out of them by then, but only just. . . He must have been about four. It wasn't through lack of trying, though, I can tell you. I always gave him what for if he made a mess.'

Melanie swallowed and stood up. 'Andrew, I need to see how much you weigh and how tall you are. Can we just slip off your coat?'

During Andrew's assessment and personal examination Melanie found him to have nits and head lice, and although there were no signs of physical or sexual abuse he did have a severe rash around his buttocks and genitals, which was probably due to the number of times he had soiled himself.

When his admission details were completed his mother announced that she had to go as her other son would be out of school. Andrew clung to her and cried.

'They've got brilliant toys here,' said Joanne as she came back into the room. 'I wish I could stay,' she added enviously.

'I don't want to stay. I want to go home,' sobbed Andrew.

'Well, you can't come home,' said his mother flatly. 'You've got to stay here, and don't let me hear you haven't been doing what you've been told, or there'll be trouble, d'you hear me?'

'I tell you what, Andrew. . .' Melanie swiftly intervened as his eyes filled with tears again. 'I have to give you a bath; would you like to come and choose some boats to play with in the water?'

At first Andrew was making too much noise to take any notice, but after she'd repeated the question he nodded.

While Andrew followed Melanie to the play area Gareth escorted his mother and sister from the ward.

Andrew's tears were soon forgotten when he saw the toys and the activities that the other children were engaged in, although he still seemed very apprehensive and clung to Melanie now that his mother had gone.

'This is Andrew,' Melanie explained to the other

children. 'We've come to find some boats for him to play with in the bath.'

After they'd chosen some toys Melanie took Andrew to the bathroom, but while she ran the bath-water the little boy sat on a stool watching, his eyes still wide with fear.

'There, the water's just right now, not too hot and not too cold,' said Melanie cheerfully. 'Let's just slip this dressing-gown off, shall we?'

Andrew shook his head.

'Come on, Andrew,' said Melanie gently. 'No one will hurt you, I promise.'

Still he seemed reluctant, his arms clutched tightly round him, firmly holding the hospital dresing-gown in place. Just as Melanie was trying to think up a different approach she realised she had not got the Malathion lotion she needed to treat Andrew's head lice. Knowing she couldn't leave him alone, she opened the bathroom door to see if there was anyone she could ask to fetch the Malathion.

The only person in sight was Gareth, who was checking some supplies in a cupboard in the corridor. He must have heard the bathroom door open, because he glanced up and saw her.

'Is anything wrong, Melanie?' he asked.

'No, not really.' She hesitated; she could hardly ask the charge nurse to fetch and carry for her.

'Is Andrew in the bath?' asked Gareth.

'Not yet—he isn't too happy with the situation, and I need to fetch something from the treatment-room. . .'

'And you want someone to stay with him. . .?'

'Please. . . Do you mind, Gareth?' This was hardly his domain either.

'Of course I don't mind.' He followed her into the bathroom and, taking one look at Andrew sitting huddled on the stool, the bath full of water, and the display of boats lined up, he immediately grasped the situation.

'Oh, wonderful — a sea battle! I haven't had one of those for ages! I just love playing dive-bombers!'

Melanie left them to it and fled to the treatment-room, where she found to her dismay that they had run out of Melathion.

By the time she returned from the store-room a good ten minutes had passed, and as she approached the bathroom she was greeted by the sound of whoops and squeals.

The little boy's eyes were shining as he gazed up at Melanie from the bath, while Gareth, who was kneeling on the floor beside him, had water dripping from his dark hair, and the front of his white coat was drenched and covered in foam.

Melanie's eyes widened, and Gareth grinned sheepishly up at her. 'Sorry, Nurse,' he said contritely, and Andrew squealed in delight.

Just for one moment Melanie was reminded of bath-times in her own home when Simon had been alive — Bath-times that, like this one, had been full of squeals and laughter, hugs and kisses.

'I'd better go now, old man —— ' Gareth scrambled to his feet ' — and let Nurse get on, otherwise I shall be in trouble.'

He grinned at Andrew, then winked at Melanie before leaving the bathroom.

After that it was easy, and as Andrew even allowed Melanie to wash his hair she decided that the ensuing mess was well worth it.

After she had dried him — very gently, so as not to aggravate his skin rash — she applied Drapolene cream, then dressed him in a pair of clean, warm hospital pyjamas that had a Paddington Bear motif.

'Do you like Paddington Bear?' she asked.

He nodded.

'Do you know the story about how he arrived on the railway station with a label round his neck?'

Andrew shook his head.

'Would you like me to tell you the story?'

He nodded again.

'Very well, I will later, before I go home, but first I have go and find some plasticine for a little girl called Catherine who is making a model of a Nativity. Would you like to come with me?'

Doubtfully he nodded again, but after she'd put his dressing-gown on he took Melanie's hand, accompanied her back to the play area, and watched with interest as she began sorting through the plasticine tin.

'Now,' she said when she had found what she wanted, 'I want you to come with me and meet Catherine. She is in bed, but she's looking forward to having you help her with her model.' She took his hand again and together they made their way down the ward to Catherine's bed.

'Hi, Catherine, this is Andrew. I told you I'd bring him to talk to you, didn't I?' Melanie smiled as Catherine looked at Andrew with interest.

'Have you come to help with my Nativity?' The little girl's gaze flew to the plasticine in Melanie's hand.

Andrew nodded.

'I'll leave you to it just for a little while,' said Melanie. 'I have a couple of jobs to do, then I'll be back to see how you are getting on.'

She was about to move away when she felt Andrew tug at her apron. For one moment she thought he was going to refuse to stay with Catherine. She glanced down and saw his expression was anxious. Maybe it was too soon to expect him to join in any activities.

'What is it, Andrew?' She bent down so that she could hear his reply, concerned he might perhaps be having the sort of problems that had brought him into hospital in the first place.

'What's a Nativity?' he whispered.

'I could have wept,' she told Gareth later when she went back to the office to report on Andrew. 'He really didn't know.'

'I'm not surprised,' replied Gareth, 'especially given the sort of background he'd come from.'

'I know. I really had to bite my tongue during his admission. I had this overwhelming urge to shake his mother.' She frowned. 'Do you ever feel like that, Gareth?'

'God, yes.' He sighed and ran his fingers through

his hair. 'I don't think I'm quite so bad as I used to be. I think to a certain extent you get used to it and are able to deal objectively with that type of case.'

'I suppose I'm finding it difficult because I've been away from nursing for so long.'

'Yes, and having two kids of your own doesn't help when it comes to being objective. It's bad enough for me sometimes, and I haven't got kids. I know once I nearly punched one guy in the mouth when I was working in Casualty.'

'Why was that?' She stared at him curiously.

'A child had been brought in with severe cigarette burns. This guy was the mother's boyfriend, and it looked pretty obvious — to me, at least — that he was responsible. I don't know how I restrained myself.'

'It would have been understandable if you had let fly at him.'

'Understandable, maybe. But totally unjustified as it turned out.'

'What do you mean?' Melanie stared him.

'It later came out in court that it was the boyfriend who had saved the child from further injury by bringing her into hospital. . .'

'Maybe, but even so. . .'

'It was the mother who had been inflicting the burns.'

'Oh, my God.' Melanie turned away, sickened.

'So it just goes to show there are two sides to every story and things are very rarely what they at first seem. The other thing we have to remember is that, no matter how bad a mother may appear to us, she is still that child's mother. As you saw with Andrew, he loves her and was very reluctant to let her go.' He glanced through the open door of his office across the ward to Andrew's bed. 'Has he settled down now?'

'Yes, he seems much happier,' she replied. 'He's made friends with Catherine and I've just told him a story.'

'Good.' He smiled, then quietly he said, 'Melanie, I won't be in tomorrow. I have to go to a meeting in Winchester, so I won't see you before Sunday.'

'Oh.' She felt an unexpected stab of disappointment. It was only Thursday, and Sunday seemed a long way off.

'I'll pick you and the children up about ten o'clock, if that's OK.'

'Yes, that will be fine.'

'Wear something warm, and make the children wear their wellies.'

'Oh?' She looked questioningly at him, expecting him to explain where they were going, but he only smiled mysteriously. For a long moment they stared at each other, and as his gaze moved from her eyes to her mouth she knew he was thinking of the moment he had kissed her.

Almost as if he had read her mind, he said, 'I hope you haven't had any second thoughts about Sunday.'

'I wouldn't dare.' She smiled. 'The children would never forgive me.'

When she arrived on the ward the following morning, Melanie found Andrew even more excited than

Catherine to see what she had found in her rummage bag.

The little girl's interest sharpened, however, when Melanie tipped out the scraps of material on to her bed, but it was Andrew who lovingly stroked the tiny pieces of velvet and lengths of gold braid for the kings' robes.

'That looks like a tea-towel.' Catherine pointed to a folded piece of striped material.

'It was a tea-towel,' said Melanie, 'but I thought it would be just right for Joseph's and the shepherds' clothes.'

Andrew was highly amused at the thought of the tiny figures they had made being dressed in tea-towels, and as Melanie hurried away to change into her uniform before report the sound of his laughter followed her down the ward.

By the time she reached the office the night sister had started giving her report. Melanie got a black look from Jean, then slipped into her seat.

After report, Sister Marder, who was in charge while Gareth was away, went through the care plans for each of the children for the coming day.

Mr Charles, the paediatrician, was coming in to see Catherine, Andrew and two other children, and there were three others for Theatre. After the day staff had received their instructions they left the office and filed back on to the ward.

'Late again, Melanie?' asked Jean sarcastically.

'As it happens, no I wasn't late. I was giving something to Catherine.'

'Catherine is my patient,' snapped Jean.

'I know that. What I was doing had nothing to do with her treatment,' explained Melanie, holding on to her temper with difficulty. 'I'm simply helping her to make a model.'

'I would have thought you had quite enough to do with the patients allocated to you without interfering with mine. I'm quite capable of giving Catherine any help she requires.'

'I honestly can't see that it matters, Jean. If there's a way any of us can help to make life more pleasant for the children, then surely it doesn't matter who does it?'

By this time they had reached the nurses' station, and Gill, another of the nurses, who was studying the notice-board suddenly swung round. 'I say, the off-duty has been changed!' she exclaimed.

'What?' Jean's eyes narrowed and she stared up at the board.

'Yes, Gareth changed it last night.' Julie Marder had come up behind them. 'He asked me to post the new list this morning, and he said if anyone had any objections they had to see him personally on Monday.'

While Julie was speaking Melanie's gaze had flown down the new list to the afternoon of the twentieth of December. To her delight she saw she was off duty, and a quick further check showed her Christmas time off had remained the same, although she was now down to work on New Year's Day.

'You got your own way, then,' sneered Jean unpleasantly. 'I suppose you went running to Gareth about it, the same as you do about everything else. It just amazes me that he puts up with it — anyone else would have been for the high jump — but then I don't suppose others go about things in quite the same way. . .' Her tone was sarcastic and suggestive.

'What's that supposed to mean?' Melanie swung round, vaguely aware that other members of staff were crowding into the tiny station behind them.

'You know damn well what it means. You've had the hots for Gareth from the moment you set eyes on him.'

'How dare you?' Melanie's eyes blazed.

'What's going on here?' Julie Marder stepped between them.

Jean swung round. 'I made it quite clear that if anyone had a problem with the off-duty list they had to see me with it and not go worrying Gareth — but no, what does she do?' She pointed to Melanie. 'She goes trotting off to Gareth at the first opportunity, flashes her eyes at him, and heaven knows what else, and gets all her own way——'

'You want to get your facts right, Jean.' They all turned as Donna suddenly stepped forward.

'What d'you mean?' Jean's eyes narrowed.

'Melanie didn't go to Gareth,' replied Donna. 'I did.'

'Why should you go?' demanded Jean, while Melanie turned to Donna in surprise.

'Because I knew that Melanie wouldn't, that's why. You've been on about Melanie being after Gareth almost from the moment she arrived; well, I can tell you straight — she isn't. I dare say Gareth fancies her something rotten — in fact it's pretty obvious that he does. . .and that's what you can't cope with, isn't it, Jean? — but Melanie isn't interested. . .'

Jean opened her mouth to retort, then a dull flush stained her features as she realised what Donna had said.

Not giving her a chance to say anything, Donna carried on, 'She wouldn't upset the system here by going to him behind your back over the off-duty, because she isn't that sort, unlike some around here. So I did it for her, because I happen to think it would be grossly unfair expecting her to work when her children are in a Nativity play.'

With a frown Julie Marder turned to Melanie. 'Is that right, Melanie?' she asked.

Melanie nodded. She could hardly trust herself to speak after Donna's outburst, aware as she was of the amused glances from the other members of staff.

'You should have said something, Melanie. We can usually work round these things, you know.' Julie turned to Jean. 'Did you know about this, Jean?'

'Of course she did,' muttered Donna.

An embarrassed silence followed, then Julie Marder said, 'I think it's time we got to work — at this rate the doctors will be here before any beds have been changed. But in future I would be obliged if you would settle any differences elsewhere and not near the ward.'

Without another word they all trooped on to the ward, but Melanie was only too aware of Jean's murderous expression.

CHAPTER TEN

As THE day wore on Melanie gradually realised just how much she was missing Gareth. She had become so used to his presence on the ward: the sheer size of him as he towered above anyone else, the warmth of his personality, his caring attitude towards the children, his humorous approach and ability to defuse any situation before it arose. . . The list was endless, but underneath all that it was simply him, Gareth, the man, she was missing.

When her shift was nearly over she sought out Donna, who was checking supplies in the treatment-room.

'Thanks for what you did earlier,' she said.

'That's OK.' Donna grinned. 'I can't bear injustice; to me it's like a red rag to a bull. It was pretty obvious that Jean was just being spiteful towards you, and anyway, it's high time she was put in her place; she's got far too high and mighty just lately.'

'Well, I suppose she is acting sister. . .'

'All the more reason for her to start learning how to manage staff and show a bit of understanding,' Donna replied sharply. 'Gareth saw the point the moment I mentioned it to him,' she added.

'What did you say to him?' Suddenly she was curious.

'Simply that your children were in some play at their school, that you were down to work, and could he please rearrange the rota. He agreed immediately, and I don't think it was just because it was you.'

'Of course it wasn't.' Melanie felt herself colour. 'I told you before. . .'

'I know what you told me. . .you aren't interested, but nothing on this earth will convince me that *he* isn't interested in *you*. You only have to watch his eyes when you are around; he follows you every-where — and that is what our friend Jean can't stand.'

'Donna. . .is there anything between them?'

'Of course not!' Donna retorted, then added darkly, 'Jean would like there to be, and she'd like everyone to think there is, but, let's face it, she just isn't Gareth's type.'

'And do you know just what is his type?'

Donna was prevented from answering by a bell ringing from the ward.

'That's Catherine,' she muttered. 'I must go to her; Jean's gone off duty.' She hurried out of the treat-ment-room, and Melanie, glancing at the clock, was glad to see it was time she too should be heading for home. It had been a long and difficult day and she was pleased it was over.

Before she left she slipped back on to the ward to see if Catherine had finished her model, but the curtains were around her bed and Melanie could hear Dr Lineham's voice from inside the cubicle.

'Melanie!'

At the sound of her name she turned and saw

Andrew. He was sitting on his bed. His mother was on one side of him, and his sister Joanne and an older boy, presumably his brother, were on the other. He looked happy. 'We finished the model,' he said excitedly.

'Good; I'm looking forward to seeing it,' said Melanie, 'but it looks as if I shall have to wait until Monday.' She glanced over her shoulder at the closed curtains.

'Are you going now?' Andrew sounded disappointed.

'Yes, but you'll be all right, Andrew; you have your family with you now.'

He sighed, then looked at his mother. 'Will you read me some Paddington story?'

The other two children looked up with interest as Andrew passed his mother the book Melanie had been reading to him.

Shirley glanced at Melanie, then opened the book and hesitantly began to read.

Unnoticed, Melanie crept away.

Sunday was one of those crisp, bright December days that so often heralded the approach of Christmas. Sophie was so excited at the prospect of a day out that Melanie had trouble restraining her. Peter was more subdued, but Melanie knew he too was looking forward to the day.

They all dressed warmly in thick sweaters, cords, anoraks and boots, and Melanie was just searching for

Sophie's mittens when a sudden shriek made her dash
from the hall into the lounge.

'For goodness' sake, Sophie, what is it now?'

'He'th here! He'th here!' Sophie, already wearing
the baseball cap Gareth had given her, was bouncing
up and down on the settee and pointing out of the
window in excitement.

Peter looked out and nodded in satisfaction. 'Good,
he's in the jeep.'

They all watched as Gareth climbed out of the jeep.
He too was dressed in cords and waxed jacket, and
today a tweed cap covered his dark hair.

He glanced towards the window as if he knew they
were there, and Melanie felt her heart lurch crazily.
All morning she had felt like a teenager preparing for
a first date. But this was madness. She was no teenager
and this was no conventional date.

With a flourish, and the air of a magician who was
sure of his audience's reaction, Gareth opened the rear
door of the jeep, and a large golden retriever jumped
to the ground.

'He'th got a dog!' With a squeal and a bump Sophie
fell off the settee.

By the time Melanie had sorted Sophie out Peter
had opened the front door and Gareth and the dog
were coming up the path.

'Hello.' His greeting was for them all, but his gaze
met Melanie's, and she felt her pulse quicken. 'I've
brought a friend to meet you — this is Monty.'

The children fussed over the dog, who sat in the

middle of the path, perfectly happy to receive any adoration that was going.

'Is he yours?' asked Melanie, wondering how Gareth managed to find the time to look after a dog.

Gareth shook his head. 'No, he belongs to my neighbour, Emily Dixon. She had a fall recently and damaged her knee. I've been helping her to exercise Monty, and I thought today should be one of those times.'

'You couldn't have thought of anything nicer.' Melanie smiled at the children's obvious delight, wishing again she could allow them to have a dog.

'Right, shall we go?' Gareth looked at each of them, and Peter nodded and ran off down the path, Sophie close behind him, holding on to Monty's lead and virtually being pulled along by the big dog.

After getting children and dog into the rear seats of the jeep, Gareth opened the passenger door for Melanie and, as she climbed into her seat, briefly she felt his hand under her elbow to assist her. It was only a small, insignificant gesture, but it reminded her of the things Simon used to do. . .things she missed now.

He took his place beside her, turned the key in the ignition, then glanced over his shoulder. 'Everyone ready?'

'Where are we going?' asked Peter.

'It'th a thurprithe!' protested Sophie, then when no one answered she added curiously, 'Where are we going, Gareth?'

He laughed. 'You really want to know?'

'Yeth.'

'I thought it might be a good idea if we went and got some new Christmas decorations — seeing that yours have got tatty.'

'The thhopth are clothed.' Sophie sounded disappointed.

'Who said anything about the shops? We're going to get proper decorations — starting with holly and ivy.'

Even Sophie fell silent at that, and Melanie smiled at Gareth's apparent ability to render her daughter speechless.

They drove west for about fifteen minutes, then Gareth drew off the dual carriageway and for the next few miles they weaved through a maze of country lanes, between rich ploughed fields bordered by hedge-rows, thick with old man's beard. Finally they entered an area of woodland, and Gareth pulled into a lay-by and switched off the engine.

They tumbled from the jeep, their breath hanging in the cold air, their feet crisp on the frosty ground. As they laughed and stamped their feet the sound of a crack from a rifle filled the air, followed by the loud cawing of rooks.

Sophie stopped dead, her eyes full of alarm. 'What wath that?'

'It's OK, Sophie,' Gareth said.

Melanie held her breath. Please don't let him mention rabbits, she prayed, or even rooks, come to that.

'I expect someone's car backfired,' he added.

'I don't think it was that. . .' began Peter, then, catching Melanie's eyes, he lapsed into silence.

'Right, troops,' said Gareth, 'here's the plan. We go through these woods, then across the fields so that Monty can have a good run, then if we come back into the woods at the top of the hill there's a good place I know where we can cut holly and ivy. Oh, and there's a prize for the one who collects the biggest pine cone.'

'Won't we get our feet wet?' asked Peter doubtfully.

'Yes, that's why I told you to wear your wellies,' replied Gareth cheerfully. 'Now come on, you guys, let's get this show on the road!'

'That'th what they thay on the telly,' giggled Sophie, then scampered on ahead with Peter and Monty.

'So is this a good idea or not?' asked Gareth as he and Melanie fell into step behind.

'It's a wonderful idea. This is just the sort of thing the children miss now. I had to sell the car after Simon died, and it's impossible to bring them to places like this. I think I've probably got over-protective of them as well,' she admitted as an afterthought.

He grinned. 'You mean over things like getting their feet wet?'

She nodded ruefully.

'That's understandable—it's a big responsibility bringing up two children on your own and trying to keep in touch with all their needs.'

'That reminds me. . .' She threw him a quick glance. 'Thanks for changing my off-duty.'

'It was no problem. I hadn't realised the date of the Nativity. What I don't understand is why you didn't come and ask me yourself.'

She hesitated. 'It was a bit delicate,' she said at last.

'What you mean is, it was Jean being bloody awkward, don't you?'

She threw him a startled glance.

'Don't worry; it isn't the first time, and it won't be the last. We're well used to it. In fact I think it's time a few changes were made on the ward.'

'Oh, please don't say anything. . . I really don't want any trouble. . . As it is, if this comes out. . . about us. . .here today. . .' She shrugged helplessly.

'What you mean is, it'll really get them going. . .us being together; is that it?' He chuckled.

She nodded.

'Of course, what they don't know is that we are only friends, that I have vowed not to lay a finger on you.' He shot her an amused look.

'Gareth. . . I'm sorry, I know I can't expect you to understand. . . No one can really understand how I feel. . . I'm not sure I understand it myself. . . It's just that I think I would feel disloyal to Simon in some way. . .if I. . .'

'It's all right,' he said softly. 'I was teasing you.'

She stared at him and, suddenly embarrassed by the amusement in his dark eyes, she was forced to look away.

In a desperate attempt to change the subject she

said, 'How did you arrange to cover my duty on the twentieth? According to Jean, there was no one else available.'

'I'm doing it,' he said simply.

She stared at him in amazement. 'You?'

'Yes. Is that so surprising?'

'No, of course not. . .although you told Sophie that you would try and get to see their Nativity as well.'

'I know I did. But I think it's far more important that their mum should be there, don't you?'

At that moment Peter came running back with a large pine cone he had found beneath the trees. 'Look, Gareth, I bet no one finds a bigger one than this.'

'I bet they do,' said Gareth.

'No, they won't; anyway, I'm going to find some more,' shouted Peter excitedly, and ran off again to join Sophie and Monty, who were rooting about under the pines.

'Talking of Nativities,' said Gareth, 'did Catherine finish her model yesterday?'

'I think so. I didn't see her when I left, because Susan Lineham was with her, but I know Andrew had been helping her. When I got home I found that Peter had made a silver star to fix over the stable; I'll take it in tomorrow.'

'That's nice.' Gareth paused. 'Do you know why Susan was with Catherine?'

'No, I'm sorry, I don't. Jean had gone by then, and Donna was looking after her.'

'I see. Any results on Andrew yet?'

'Not really; Mr Charles is still running tests. He

had Andrew on a very high-fibre diet and a fibre supplement, but he hasn't ruled out an obstruction yet.'

'Poor little chap. Let's hope it's nothing like that. Was he any happier on Friday?'

'Yes, I think so,' she replied slowly. 'I had to work at it, but I think I won him round in the end. But it was helping Catherine that really saved the day,' she added, then glanced up sharply at a shout from Sophie.

'Mum. . .my! Monty'th all wet!'

Gareth grinned. 'He'll have been in the stream at the edge of the field.'

'You've obviously been here before.'

'Yes, I often bring Monty up here.'

'You say he belongs to your neighbour?' She glanced curiously at him.

'Yes,' he replied. 'I rent the cottage next to hers, and she's come to rely on my exercising Monty since her fall. You'll meet her later if you come to watch me play rugby—she'll come to the ground to pick Monty up. You are coming to watch, aren't you?'

She laughed. 'Try keeping Sophie away.'

Suddenly Melanie realised how little she knew about him and was consumed with curiosity—about where he lived, the type of life he led, and even about the poor old soul who lived next door to him and who had come to rely on him to exercise her dog.

After Monty had had a good run they backtracked into the woods, where Gareth cut the greenery, then with their arms full they made their way back to the jeep. Everyone's pockets were stuffed with pine cones and, while Sophie spread them out on the ground in four piles so that Gareth could judge who had the biggest, Melanie thought how lovely they would look on her mantelpiece.

Peter won the prize, and as Gareth produced a Mars bar from his pocket Sophie began to sulk.

'I'm hungry. . .' she wailed.

'In that case, it must be time for lunch,' replied Gareth. 'I know a nice little pub near here that does an excellent Sunday lunch.'

'A pub. . .?' Peter's eyes had grown enormous, and Sophie forgot she was supposed to be sulking.

'Yes,' said Gareth firmly, then, glancing at Melanie, he said, 'They have a good children's room.'

'All right.' She nodded weakly. She'd never taken the children to a pub before. But it seemed that since they'd met Gareth they were doing all sorts of things they hadn't done before.

The pub turned out to be a picturesque inn in a small village on the far side of the woods. The landlord greeted them by throwing another log on the roaring fire and giving them a menu to peruse while he served their drinks.

Even Sophie seemed overawed by her new surroundings, or maybe she was simply tired after all the exercise, but she and Peter sat quietly in a high-backed alcove seat with Monty at their feet and sipped tall glasses of orange juice.

And it was in that moment, as they warmed themselves before the open fire, that Melanie was suddenly overcome by a feeling of how right it felt to be here with Gareth and her children, just as if they were a family, like any of the other countless families across the country who were also enjoying a Sunday in each other's company.

She set her glass on the table, leaned her head against the high back of her seat, and sighed with contentment. Glancing up, she found Gareth watching her.

'You look lovely,' he said softly. 'The fresh air has brought a glow to your cheeks. You also look happy,' he added.

'I am,' she admitted. 'Very happy.'

'Mum! Did you see that? That was Gareth who scored!' Peter was jumping up and down in excitement on the touchline, while Sophie, unable to contain herself, was whistling continuously through her fingers in the way that Gareth had taught her on the way to the rugby field.

Melanie had long since given up trying restrain them, and even she had begun to enjoy the game, although, if she was honest, it was only Gareth she was really watching.

Gareth, his powerful body in shorts and striped shirt, his dark hair damp and tousled, was becoming more and more mud-spattered with every passing minute.

She became so engrossed in the game, joining the children in their encouragement, that she jumped in surprise when someone touched her arm.

She turned sharply and found a young, attractive girl at her side.

The girl looked in her early twenties and had green eyes and rich chestnut hair that tumbled on to her shoulders. She was leaning heavily on an elbow crutch.

'Hello,' she said, 'you must be Melanie. I'm Emily Dixon, Gareth's neighbour.'

Melanie stared at her in astonishment.

From Gareth's description she had pictured Emily Dixon as a frail little old lady with brittle bones. If she was in any further doubt as to the girl's identity it was dispelled by Monty, who leapt up and gave his mistress a rapturous welcome.

'Are you having a good time?' The girl glanced at Peter and Sophie. 'It's awfully good of you to take Monty out. I really didn't know how I was going to manage to exercise him when I had my accident.'

'Your accident. . .?' Melanie glanced at the elbow crutch.

'Yes, I had a fall while I was hunting. . .' The girl pulled a face.

'Oh, I see,' said Melanie faintly, finally banishing preconceived images of old ladies falling on garden paths.

Peter and Sophie meanwhile had lost interest in the newcomer and turned back to the game.

'Gareth's been marvellous,' the girl went on. 'I don't know what I would have done without him. We often do this, you know—he takes Monty for a really long run, then he brings him here and I come down in my car to pick Monty up while Gareth's playing. Do you like rugby. . .?'

Before Melanie could answer, Sophie turned round again. 'I do,' she said and, staring suspiciously up at the newcomer as if she had just recognised a possible rival for Gareth's affections, she added, 'Gareth'th my friend.'

'I know he is.' Emily laughed, showing very white, even teeth. 'He's told me all about you.'

'Has he?' Melanie wondered what he'd told her.

Had he misled this girl as well—just as he had misled her by allowing her to believe his neighbour was elderly and infirm? Had he told her that he felt sorry for them—the woman he worked with whose husband had been tragically killed, leaving her with two small children?

Was that how he saw them?

She had thought he was interested in her, had even put him off because she wasn't ready, but had she misinterpreted the situation?

Both Donna and Jenny had said he was interested in her, but what if they'd been wrong? What if he had simply been being kind to them all?

But wasn't that what she had wanted?

In sudden confusion she stared across the field, her eye immediately picking Gareth out of the knot of players.

What if he was romantically involved with this attractive redhead at her side? Would it matter?

And it was then that she knew that yes, it would matter.

Gradually she became aware that Emily was talking again and she hadn't heard a word she'd been saying.

'I'm sorry.' She frowned. 'What did you say?'

The girl smiled. 'Only that I was going. Tell Gareth I'll see him later.'

Miserably she watched as the girl walked across the field to her car, Monty ambling along at her side, tired now after all his exercise.

'Who was that?' She turned and found Peter at her side. He too was staring after the girl.

'Monty's mistress,' she explained, hoping at the same time she was only Monty's mistress and not anyone else's.

'I know that. But who is she? Is she Gareth's girlfriend?' Suddenly even Peter sounded suspicious, and in spite of the way she was feeling Melanie was forced to hide a smile.

'I don't know,' she admitted.

To Sophie's delight Gareth's team won. They waited in the jeep while he showered and changed, then on the way home to Winchester Close he stopped at a garden centre and bought them a Christmas tree.

While Gareth and Peter unloaded the jeep Melanie and Sophie went indoors and made tea and toasted crumpets.

Gareth stayed until the children were in bed, but when Melanie came downstairs he stood up, as if preparing to leave.

'Do you have to go?'

She wanted him to stay. More than anything she

wanted him to stay. But she didn't know how to tell him.

'Yes, I must get home. I have things to do.'

Emily had said to tell him she would see him later. She hadn't told him. . .hadn't been able to bring herself to do so, even to mention the red-haired girl with the green eyes.

'Besides,' he went on, unaware of what she was thinking, 'I don't want to outstay my welcome. You'll have had quite enough of me today.' He looked down at her.

She hadn't had enough of him. She didn't want him to go.

She looked up and met his gaze, remembering the time he had kissed her, remembering all the fire and passion that had been in that kiss. Surely she hadn't imagined that?

He took a step towards her. He was going to kiss her again. What would she do this time? Would she reject him again?

No. Suddenly she knew without any doubt that this time she wouldn't. This time it would be what she wanted. She felt herself tense, waiting, longing for him to touch her, to feel his arms around her, his mouth on hers.

'Melanie. . .'

'Yes?'

He hesitated. . .then took a deep breath and stepped back. 'I had better be going,' he muttered.

'But——' she began.

'No, it's best I go.'

She heard herself thank him politely for a lovely day, heard herself say goodbye, watched him go out of the house. She saw him get into the jeep and drive away to go to a girl called Emily.

She had been wrong. She had misread his intentions. He did only feel sorry for her and the children.

With a sob she closed the front door and leaned against it, closing her eyes.

CHAPTER ELEVEN

'WHERE were you, for heaven's sake? I tried phoning several times.' Jenny stared at them across her kitchen as Melanie and the children arrived the following morning.

'We went to a pub!' announced Sophie before Melanie had a chance even to open her mouth. 'With Gareth,' she added triumphantly.

'Did you, now?' Jenny turned to Melanie, a gleam of speculation in her eye.

'It wasn't what you're thinking,' muttered Melanie.

'How do you know what I'm thinking?' Jenny maddeningly raised her eyebrows and looked down at Sophie. 'Did you have a lovely time, poppet?'

'Ooh, yeth.' Sophie sighed. 'I had a knickerbocker glory for my pudding.'

'And Gareth bought us a Christmas tree,' Peter chipped in excitedly.

'And he'th got a dog called Monty. . .'

'And we went to the woods and collected fir cones and holly and watched him play rugby. . .'

'My, my, you have had a wonderful time.' Jenny smiled. 'And what about Mummy? Did she have a wonderful time as well?'

'Oh, yeth,' said Sophie solemnly. 'Gareth told her she looked lovely and she thaid she wath very happy.'

'Well, isn't that nice.' Jenny grinned at Melanie.

'You can take that silly look off your face,' said Melanie, but she was forced to smile, in spite of the way she was feeling.

'I must go,' she said after a frantic glance at the clock. 'I shall miss my bus, then I shall be late and I'll be in trouble. Even Gareth won't forgive me for that. . .'

'Oh, I don't know. . .' Jenny began, then ducked as Melanie picked up a tea-towel and threw it at her.

She wasn't late; in fact she was ten minutes early. She knew Gareth was in his office, because his jeep was parked in its usual place in the car park.

Neither Jean nor Donna had arrived, and on a sudden wild impulse she thought she would go and see Gareth, had to see him, even if it was only to thank him again for taking them out.

She had hardly slept the night before for thinking about him, and when she had eventually dropped off her dreams had been full of him.

She had even dreamt he had made love to her, and it had been wonderful. . . Maybe her sister was right and it was time she started living her life again. . . Maybe it wouldn't be disloyal to Simon if she found happiness in another man's arms. . . Maybe that was what Simon would have wanted her to do. . .

Suddenly her need to see Gareth became desperate, to find out once and for all whether she had misread his intentions towards her or whether the tenderness in his eyes and the passion in that kiss had been the real thing.

Some sixth sense was warning her that if she dallied around too long she would never have the chance to find out. Gareth was far too attractive and, even if Jean didn't seem to constitute a serious threat, there was still the glamorous neighbour who seemed only too willing.

She hurried down the corridor, straightening her cap as she went, then, pausing briefly before his office door, she tapped lightly, then turned the handle and pushed open the door.

He was standing with his back to her and appeared to be gazing out of the window.

'Gareth,' she began, 'I wanted to see you. . .'

She expected him to turn at the sound of her voice, but he didn't. 'Gareth. . .?'

He turned then and, although instinct had warned her something was wrong, she was unprepared when she saw that his cheeks were wet with tears.

'Gareth, what is it?' She came right into the office and closed the door behind her.

He stared at her for a long moment, then in a choked voice that was nothing like his own he said, 'It's Catherine — she died last night.'

For a long moment they simply stared at each other, then Melanie moved forward and put her arms round him, holding him against her.

'I'm so sorry,' she whispered at last.

'It's silly, I know,' he said in a muffled voice. 'I

should be used to this sort of thing by now, but this has really got to me.'

'What happened?' Still she held him.

'She had a severe reaction to her chemotherapy. Her little body just couldn't take any more. Apparently she started to deteriorate on Friday night. . . Her family moved in here and were all with her.' He swallowed, was silent for a moment, then went on, 'She slipped into a coma yesterday afternoon, then died late last night.'

So while they had been laughing and enjoying themselves the previous day, little Catherine had been fighting for her life.

'I'm sorry, Melanie.' Gareth straightened up and wiped his face with the back of his hand. 'I didn't mean anyone to see me like this.'

'I'm not anyone; I'm me——' she began, then stopped as the phone rang on his desk. She watched as he spoke to someone, listened, then replaced the receiver.

'We have to go,' he said briskly. 'Casualty are sending up a child who has been involved in a road traffic accident. I need to get on to the orthopaedic registrar.'

The next hour passed in a blur as the rest of the staff arrived and had to be told about Catherine. There was a great deal of distress as each person reacted to the news.

After report Melanie went on to the ward and found Andrew bursting with excitement.

'I've been waiting for you,' he said. 'Look!' He pointed to the end of the ward.

Melanie turned, and there in the centre of a shelf above Catherine's empty bed stood the completed model of the Nativity.

'I finished it!' Andrew exclaimed in triumph. 'Catherine didn't feel very well — I think she had a headache — so I finished it. Go and have a look.'

Swallowing the lump that had suddenly risen in her throat, Melanie crossed the ward and, through a blur of tears, looked at the tiny figures dressed in the scraps of material from her rummage bag.

She slipped her hand into her uniform pocket and drew out the silver star Peter had made. He had attached it to a thin piece of wire, and she stuck the end into a lump of plasticine so that the star hung directly over the stable.

For a long moment she stood and stared at it, fighting her tears.

'She went home,' Andrew called across the ward. 'She went home and she forgot to take the model with her.'

Taking a deep breath, Melanie picked the model up and walked back to Andrew's bed.

'No, Andrew,' she said firmly, 'I don't think she forgot it at all. Do you know what I think?'

'No.' His eyes widened as he stared up at her.

'I think she left it for you,' she said softly, and placed it on his bedspread.

★　★　★

Sarah, the child involved in the road traffic accident, was very badly injured. She had suffered a fractured pelvis and right femur, a ruptured spleen and much bruising and laceration of the skin on her face and legs.

Melanie and Donna spent most of the morning tending to her, taking her to X-ray, calming her distraught father, who had been driving the car in which she had been a passenger, and coping with her mother, who had hysterics when she arrived and caught sight of her daughter.

Sarah's parents started arguing over whose fault the accident had been, Andrew began crying because he'd soiled his bed, and the radio at the end of the ward blared out the latest chart-topper.

'There's never a dull moment on this ward, is there?' said Donna, catching Melanie's eye as they straightened Sarah's bedclothes.

Melanie had no further chance to speak to Gareth until almost the end of her shift, then, just as she was preparing to go off duty and thought she might be able to have a word with him she was waylaid in the corridor by Andrew's mother, Shirley.

'Nurse——' the woman looked harassed and tired '—can I speak to you, please?'

'Yes, of course.' Out of the corner of her eye Melanie could see Gareth putting his jacket on. If she didn't hurry, she would miss him.

'Andrew says you're his special nurse.'

'Yes, that's right, I have been assigned to look after Andrew,' she replied.

'Well, perhaps you could tell me what I should do. I'm worried, you see.' Shirley pushed her lank hair out of her eyes.

At that moment Gareth came out of his office and looked towards them.

'Everything all right, Staff?' he asked.

Suddenly all she wanted to do was to grab her coat and go with him. He still looked sad, and she knew Catherine's death had affected him badly. He needed someone.

Wildly she looked at Shirley, wondering if she could put her off, tell her she would speak to her the following day. Instead she heard herself, quite calmly, say 'Everything's fine, thanks, Gareth. Shirley and I are just going to have a little chat about Andrew.'

'In that case I'll be off.' He nodded to them both and helplessly she watched as he left the ward, the swing-doors closing behind him.

With a little sigh she pulled herself together. 'Come into the office,' she said to Shirley. 'We can talk in there without being disturbed.'

'So what's the problem?' she asked a moment later as Shirley sat down opposite her.

'I've just spoken to Dr Lineham about Andrew's tests.' The woman sniffed, and Melanie wondered if she was about to hear another piece of bad news.

'She said he was OK, that he could probably go home at the end of the week — once they've sorted his food out, you know.'

'But that's marvellous, Shirley—you must be so pleased.'

'You don't understand.' Shirley looked at the floor. 'I think he's going to be put into care.'

Melanie stared at her. 'Are you sure?' she asked at last, trying to imagine how she would have felt in the same situation, and failing miserably.

'Not absolutely,' Shirley mumbled, 'but it was that social worker—she as good as said that was what would happen with Andrew. She said I wasn't fit to look after him. . .nosy cow!'

'And do you think you are, Shirley?' asked Melanie quietly.

'I'm his mother, aren't I?' she flashed back.

'Yes, you are, and in my book that makes you the best possible person to look after him. But you have had problems, haven't you, Shirley?' she said gently. 'Andrew has had problems—serious problems that brought him in here in the first place.'

The woman fell silent and looked at the floor again.

'Can you tell me about those problems?' asked Melanie after a while.

'It all got on top of me after me husband left. . . I couldn't cope. . . I just let everything go. . . I know the kids suffered. . .but they're still my kids. . . I still care about them.'

Shirley looked up sharply, and Melanie saw that her eyes were bright with unshed tears. 'It'd kill Andrew if he had to go into care. . . He wants to come home with me. . .' She swallowed and trailed off.

'I know, Shirley. I know he does. Do you think you'd be able to cope better now?'

She nodded. 'I'm sure I would. I've even given up me job to be with the kids more. . .'

'Well, in that case I'll have a word with the charge nurse and see if he can do anything for you,' said Melanie firmly. 'I can't promise anything, but I'll do my best.'

'Thank you, Nurse.' Shirley wiped her hand across her eyes. 'Andrew was right—you are special.'

By the time she left Shirley, Gareth was long gone, and all Melanie could do was to go and fetch the children from her sister.

'You don't look very happy,' remarked Jenny as she let her in. 'What's up?'

'I've had one hell of a day.'

'Never mind, you're off tomorrow for the Nativity—Sophie's so excited I don't know what to do with her.'

As if to confirm her words, Sophie suddenly burst into the kitchen, her eyes shining, her cheeks flushed. 'I'm going to be an ath, I'm going to be an ath,' she chanted as she danced around the room. 'Gareth'th coming to watch me, Gareth'th coming to watch me. . .'

'Sophie, Sophie, please calm down.' Melanie caught her daughter as she danced past. 'And I'm afraid Gareth won't be coming to watch you.'

The little girl stopped dead and stared at her, and

even Jenny turned from the sink, where she was peeling vegetables for the evening meal.

'He thaid he would. . .' Sophie began.

'He said he would go if he possibly could. . . Well, unfortunately he is having to cover for me, so that I can go.'

'He thaid he'd come and watch me!' Sophie's bottom lip dropped into a pout.

'I know, but——'

'He will!' shouted Sophie, and rushed from the room.

'Oh, dear, that's torn it,' said Jenny. 'She's been going on about him being there all afternoon.'

Melanie shrugged helplessly. 'There's nothing I can do about it.'

'She's really taken with him, isn't she?'

'Yes, I suppose she is,' agreed Melanie.

'And what about you? Are you really taken with him as well?'

'Oh, Jenny, I think I must be.' To her horror she felt her eyes fill with tears, and she sank down on to the nearest chair.

With an exclamation Jenny flung down the vegetable knife, crossed the kitchen, and put her arm round her.

'Oh, Mel, what is it? What's wrong?'

'I don't know—it's all suddenly such a muddle.' She gulped and wiped her eyes with a tissue.

'I don't see why,' said Jenny slowly. 'It certainly seemed as if he was keen on you.'

'I thought so. . .but now I'm not so sure. . . I think

he may have just been being kind because he felt sorry for us.'

'Oh, surely not. Whatever makes you think that?' Jenny stared at her.

'I don't know; it was just a feeling I had. . .and. . . and then there's this girl, you see. . .and I'm not sure where she fits in.'

'What girl? That nurse you told me about on your ward?'

'No, no,' said Melanie quickly, 'not her, not Jean. I know he isn't interested in Jean, but there's this other girl, Emily; she's his neighbour, and they seem very friendly indeed. . .'

'Do you think you put him off when you told him you weren't ready for another relationship?' asked Jenny.

'Yes, I think I probably did,' replied Melanie miserably. 'People just don't understand, Jen, how hard it is. . .'

'Maybe he did, maybe he didn't,' said Jenny, 'but I think it's high time you let him know how you feel about him.'

'I don't know when I'm going to do that. I'm not sure of his duties now. I may not see him again until after Christmas!' She stared at Jenny in dismay.

The children from the nursery class and from the primary school had joined together to produce the Nativity play, which was to be performed in the local church. When Melanie and Jenny arrived the pews were rapidly filling up with parents and friends, but ιt last they managed to find a space fairly near the front.

'Doesn't the church look lovely?' whispered Jenny. 'All that greenery and those candles! I love Christmas; it's my favourite time of year.'

Melanie was about to reply that she used to love Christmas at one time but that it would never be the same again. But something stopped her, and, biting her lip, she remained silent. For although she might have felt that way until very recently, now a little of the old magic had started to creep back.

As if to endorse her feelings, two columns of children, dressed as shepherds, townsfolk and animals, their faces shining in the light from the candles, began to walk up the aisle.

A stable had been built at the chancel steps, complete with crib, and as Mary and Joseph took their places a little choir of angels with gauze wings and silver tinsel haloes began singing 'Away In A Manger'.

Melanie blinked and swallowed, thinking of Catherine, of how she had wanted to be an angel and of the pleasure she'd had in making the model Nativity.

Jenny nudged her elbow, and she looked up.

'Look——' Jenny nodded towards the altar '—there's Peter.'

Melanie craned her neck and was just able to see her son as he stepped forward to give the news to the shepherds. Then her attention was taken by a frantic movement from the foot of the chancel steps, and she

saw a little figure with a ass's mask hopping from e
foot to another in a desperate attempt to be seen.

Jenny's younger daughter, Cassie, read one of the
lessons, and as the choir sang 'Silent Night' the full
power of the Christmas message washed over Melanie.

Just before she sat down again, something
prompted her to look round.

Gareth was standing at the back of the church, head
and shoulders above everyone else, and he was looking
directly at her. As their eyes met he inclined his head.

He had come. How he had managed it, she had no
idea, but he had made a promise to Sophie, and he
had kept it. With a little sigh she turned to the front
again.

Jenny threw her a puzzled glance, then she too
looked over her shoulder. A moment later she was
chuckling softly.

Half an hour later, after the three kings had put in
their appearance and the play drew to its conclusion,
the little band once more made its way down the aisle.

This time as a certain little creature made its way
past their pew it looked towards them and in a loud
stage whisper said, 'Gareth'th here. I told you he'd
come.'

It took a long time for the children to file into the
school building next door, and even longer for their
parents to leave the church. By the time Melanie and
Jenny reached the porch, to Melanie's dismay there
was no sign of Gareth.

They waited for several minutes, the cold
December wind whipping round their ankles, attack-

noses and fingers, and whirling dead leaves into
he corners of the porch.

At last they were joined by the excited children.

'Did you see Gareth?' asked Peter excitedly.

'You thed he wouldn't come!' accused Sophie
triumphantly.

Melanie smiled. 'I know I did; I'm sorry, but I
thought he had to work. He took my place so that I
could come and see you in the play. I don't know how
he managed to get here.'

'I do,' said Peter. 'I spoke to him on the way out.'

Melanie looked sharply at him. 'Did you? What did
he say?'

'He said he'd managed to get an hour off, but that
was all, and he had to go straight back to the hospital.
He said to tell you that he was sorry he couldn't wait.'

'Oh!' Sophie pouted. 'I wanted to thee if he liked
my mathk. . . Did you like my mathk?' She looked
up at Melanie.

'Yes, darling.' Melanie bent down and gave her a
quick hug. 'I loved your mask. You were the best
little donkey I've ever seen.'

'I wathen't a donkey. I wath an ath!' protested
Sophie as they made their way to Jenny's car.

'And you were doubting how he felt?' murmured
Jenny as she unlocked the car and the children
scrambled into the rear seat.

Melanie smiled as she took her own place. 'He must
have gone to all sorts of trouble to get that hour off —
I know how difficult it is on the ward at the moment —
and I can't even phone him to thank him. Do you

know something, Jenny? I don't even know where lives!'

'I know where he lives,' said a voice from the rear seat of the car.

Melanie and Jenny looked at each other, then Melanie turned her head and looked between the front seats. 'What did you say, Peter?' she said slowly.

'I said I know where Gareth lives.'

'But how do you know?'

'He told me when he asked me if I wanted to go fishing with him. He lives in one of those cottages behind the playing fields near the river.'

'Yeth,' agreed Sophie solemnly. 'Number thix.'

Melanie and Jenny looked at each other, then burst out laughing.

CHAPTER TWELVE

IT WAS a clear night, the shops were still brightly lit to attract late shoppers, and a Salvation Army band was playing carols in Woolworth's doorway as Melanie drove Jenny's car through the town. The recreation grounds and playing fields were on the far side of town, and the cottages were on the tow-path beside the river that separated the water-meadows.

Melanie's heart was beating very fast as she parked the car, and by the time she had walked along the tow-path and found number six she had almost chickened out.

The cottage was one of a pair—whitewashed, beneath a slate roof and with a black-studded front door. It appeared to be in darkness. With a trembling hand she lifted the knocker and let it fall.

A light came on in the glass fanlight above the door, and Melanie heard someone turn the catch. As the door opened she swallowed and stepped back.

Emily Dixon stood in the open doorway.

Melanie stared at her in shocked dismay. What was she doing there? Had there been much more to Gareth's relationship with his attractive young neighbour than she had realised? Even as the thoughts chased each other round in her mind she became aware that Emily was also staring at her in a shocked sort of way.

The other girl was the first to speak. Trying to lc
past Melanie as if she expected to see someone els
she said, 'Is Gareth with you?'

'Gareth?' Melanie frowned. What in the world was
she talking about? 'No, why should he be?' She shook
her head. 'I was hoping to find him here.' It was her
turn to look past Emily into the lighted hallway.

'Oh, you must have crossed on the way!' The girl
gave a peal of laughter and, flicking back her chestnut
hair, she stood aside. 'You'd better come in and
wait—I shouldn't think he would be too long when
he finds you're not there.'

Silently Melanie followed her into the cottage,
through the hallway into a bright, cosy kitchen.

'Are you saying Gareth has gone to see me?' she
asked slowly as Emily turned to face her.

'Yes, he's taken Monty with him—I just brought
him some fruit cake I'd made. I told him he'd better
make the most of it; I won't have much time for
baking after the weekend.'

'The weekend?'

'My fiancé, Dave, will be home,' she explained.
'He's a marine biologist. . . We're getting married at
Easter.'

'Your fiancé. . .?' said Melanie faintly. 'Then you
and Gareth. . .you aren't. . .?'

'Gareth?' The girl pealed with laughter again. 'Good
heavens, no. Is that what you thought?' Her eyes
suddenly narrowed. 'Oh, my God! No wonder things
have been difficult.'

'What do you mean, "difficult"?' Melanie frowned,

at the same time was aware of an overwhelming
ense of relief that this girl wasn't romantically linked
to Gareth in any way.

'I was beginning to think you two were never going
to get together.' Emily smiled, then glanced at the
clock on the dresser. 'Look, I'm afraid I shall have to
dash — I'm expecting a phone call from Dave. . . Do
you mind?'

'Of course not. I'll just wait.' Melanie watched
Emily as she limped to the back door then paused,
one hand on the catch, and looked back.

'I tell you what.' She grinned. 'I'm jolly glad I'm
not interested in Gareth — he's so besotted with you, I
don't think he's even aware of anyone else.'

With a wave of her hand she was gone, and weakly
Melanie sank down on a chair to wait.

Gareth stood in the open doorway and stared at her in
amazement.

'Melanie! What the —— ?'

'Emily let me in,' she explained quickly.

'But what are you doing here? I've just been to see
you.'

'I know. Why did you want to see me?'

He stared at her for a long moment, and something
in his expression made her bones feel as if they had
turned to water.

'Because I couldn't stand it any longer,' he said
simply at last.

'You couldn't stand what?'

'This messing around over the way I feel about

you. . . I know I said I wouldn't rush you, but I'm sorry, Melanie, I can't help it. . . I can't wait any longer. . .' In two strides he was across the room and had gathered her up into his arms, whirling her round then setting her down and bringing his mouth down to cover hers. When at last they drew apart she was breathless.

'Oh, Gareth. . .' Weakly she clung to him.

Taking hold of her coat collar, he forced her to look up into his eyes. 'So why did you come here?' he said softly.

'What? Oh, it doesn't really matter now. . .' she murmured.

'Oh, yes, it does. I want to know.' His grip tightened, and she laughed.

'All right, if you insist. I was going to tell you that I may have been silly in saying I wasn't ready to start another relationship. . . I came to the conclusion that I shall never know if I don't try. . .'

She was silenced by yet another kiss, a long, lingering kiss this time, with more than a hint of the smouldering passion she had suspected before.

'You see,' she finally went on, when she pulled away from him, 'I do realise how difficult it must be for anyone who hasn't "been there", so to speak, to understand how it feels——'

'Melanie,' he interrupted gently.

'Yes?'

'Do you remember the first time you said that to me?'

She frowned, and, not giving her a chance to

swer, he continued, 'And I said that maybe I understood far better than you thought.'

She nodded slowly.

'Well, I think it's high time I set the record straight and tell you what I meant.' He glanced at his watch. 'Do you have to hurry back?'

She shook her head.

'The children?'

'They're staying with my sister.'

'All night?' Amusement glittered in his dark eyes, and she felt colour touch her cheeks as she nodded.

'In that case,' he said softly, 'I suggest we make ourselves more comfortable, and I'll tell you about Kim.'

Taking her hand, he led her into a sitting-room with old-fashioned overhead oak beams, and thick velvet curtains that shut out the cold December night.

He put a match to the fire, and within minutes blue flames were licking the pine logs in the hearth.

They lingered for a moment, standing in front of the fire while he kissed her again, then he drew her down beside him on to the sofa and gathered her into his arms.

'Who was Kim?' she asked at last.

He remained silent for a long moment, and just when she was beginning to wonder if he had changed his mind he slowly began, 'Kim was the girl I was going to marry.'

She stared at him in astonishment. At first she'd thought it might have been Jean, then Emily, now here he was about to tell her of his love for a girl named Kim.

He stared into the fire, watching the flames as they took hold and leaped and flickered around the logs.

'I met Kim at polytechnic,' he said at last, his voice sounding strange, husky, as if it pained him to talk of her. 'We fell in love and we moved in together. We lived together for two years, and we were so happy. . . Then Kim started to develop stomach problems.'

He swallowed, was silent for a further minute, then continued, 'Eventually she saw a consultant, and she was taken into hospital in Cardiff for investigation. She was found to have a massive stomach tumour. . .' He paused, and Melanie turned her head.

All she could see in the firelight was his profile, but from the emotion in his voice she could sense rather than see the tears in his eyes.

'They operated immediately, and at first all seemed well. She started a course of treatment, but it made her so ill. . . I used to sit with her for hours. . .just sit there, quietly, you know?'

He threw Melanie an anxious glance, and when she nodded, understanding, he went on, 'Anyway, gradually she got weaker; more surgery was out of the question. We were told it was just a matter of time. I gave up my course so that I could be with her. . . She died in my arms six months later. . .' His voice cracked and he trailed off.

'Oh, Gareth,' she whispered, drawing him closer to her.

'It's hell, isn't it, afterwards?' he said a few moments later.

'Why didn't you tell me before?' Melanie lifted her hand and with one finger gently traced a line down his cheek and across his lips.

'I couldn't. You had enough to be getting on with with your own problems, without my burdening you with mine.' As he spoke he grasped her hand and kissed her fingers one by one.

'It might have helped,' she said slowly. 'If I knew you'd been through the same sort of thing, I would at least have known you understood my feelings. . . As it was, I thought no one understood. . . I even wondered if it was just that you felt sorry for me. . .'

'Oh, Melanie, I wish I had told you now. . . Hindsight's a wonderful thing, isn't it?' He gave a rueful smile, and she felt her heart constrict.

'Most definitely,' she agreed. For the first time since Simon's death she felt she had found someone who truly understood.

They remained silent for a long time, then curiously she turned her head and looked at him. 'You said you gave up your course; did you mean nursing?'

'No.' He shook his head. 'I left home to study electronics, because I didn't want to follow my father and brothers down the mine — that's what I was studying at the poly. Kim was on a business studies course. It was only after she died that I decided on nursing.'

'Did her illness influence you?'

'Yes.' There was no hesitation in his voice. 'I

thought while Kim was ill that it was just because of her that I wanted to nurse her, and at the start it probably was, but as time went on I became convinced it was what I wanted to do for the rest of my life.'

'Why paediatrics?'

'I've always loved kids—I come from a big family. . . It felt right, that's all.'

'Catherine really got to you, didn't she?' she said quietly.

He nodded. 'Yes, she did. Her case was so similar to Kim's, you see. It really made me think, Melanie— about us, I mean. . . Life's so short. . . We just have to get on with it.'

They fell silent again, each reflecting on other times, other places, other loves, then quietly Gareth said, 'I thought I shouldn't rush you, Melanie, thought there was no point until you were sure you were ready, because I knew how you felt.

'But Catherine's dying seemed to trigger something, then seeing you and the children today at the service. . . It was all so moving, and now. . .now I want you to know that I love you. I want to take care of you, and Peter, and Sophie, if you'll let me. You've been on your own long enough; you need someone to care for you, to love you.'

'You think I'm not capable of taking care of myself and the children?' There was humour in the accusing note in her voice.

'I wouldn't dare suggest it.' He grinned suddenly. 'In fact, if I'm honest I think you cope admirably, but

I still think you could be happier if you would only let me show you how. Will you, Melanie?'

'Yes, Gareth,' she whispered, then added, 'I love you too. I can hardly believe it, but it's true. For a long while I thought if I let myself love you it would in some way be disloyal to Simon. Now I realise it would be what Simon would want. He loved life and he loved me; he wouldn't have wanted me to be miserable for the rest of my life, or for the children to grow up without a father.'

Fiercely he pulled her closer, then slowly, gently, he aroused her, softly caressing, whispering words of love, displaying an unbelievable depth of tenderness, as if he was still afraid of rushing her, of hurting her, of having her pull away again and tell him she wasn't ready.

Only this time she was ready and, far from offering any resistance as he slowly undressed her, she found herself wanting him with a desire that shocked and amazed her—a desire that came from deep in her soul, a desire she hadn't felt for such a very long time, a desire she'd thought had died with Simon.

And suddenly even that felt different. Simon had been different; she had loved him, wanted him, but that had been then.

This was now, this was Gareth, and she knew without a shadow of doubt that she now wanted him, loved him, as much as she had once wanted Simon.

With a little sigh she raised her hips as he slid the last of her clothes from her body, watched him as he undressed, the firelight flickering on the big, muscular body. She lay back, waiting for him, and he knelt down beside her, then, lifting her in his arms, he moved her from the sofa to the sheepskin rug in front of the fire.

'You are so lovely, Melanie.'

With gentle caresses, butterfly kisses, he adored every inch of her, and at the moment of piercing sweetness when he finally entered her body she knew she was his for all time.

For him the moment seemed to herald the end of restraint, and it was as if he could hold back no longer.

For Melanie, too, the barriers were down, and she rose and fell to meet the rhythm of his love. Moments later they soared together.

Later, as they lay together in the glow from the dying embers of the fire, Gareth suddenly chuckled.

'What is it?' She raised her head and looked down at him.

'I was just thinking, it can take some couples half a lifetime to achieve what we just did.'

'In that case it must be right.'

'I have no doubts about that.' Softly, after a moment's hesitation, he said, 'Do you?'

'No, not now.' She smiled, then grew serious. 'But it could be easier for me in the long run than for you, Gareth.'

'You mean because of the children?'

'Exactly. . . It isn't everyone who would want to take on a ready-made family.'

A far-away look came into his eyes. 'I always wanted

a son,' he mused. 'Someone to go fishing with. . .' He paused. 'I was going to say, "Someone to play rugby with", but on second thoughts I think that could probably be Sophie rather than Peter. . .'

Melanie laughed. 'You could well be right there. Peter has never been into sport, but that could be something to do with losing his father. . . I don't know. . .'

'I know one thing I shall have to do,' said Gareth suddenly.

'Oh, what's that?'

'Take up stamp-collecting again.'

'You would do that?'

'Of course. Peter must never know. . .' He trailed off, then threw her an anxious glance. 'Do you think there could be a problem with Peter?' he asked slowly.

'There might be,' she replied. 'I'm not sure. I think he saw you as a threat at one time, but now I don't know. . .but, believe it or not, it was Peter who told me where you lived. . .'

'Ah, was it, now? I wondered how you knew.' He chuckled, and hugged her more tightly.

'Yes.' She hesitated, unsure how to go on, and a log suddenly fell apart, sending sparks shooting up the chimney.

'Wait a minute. . .' He eased himself away from her and, lifting his head, he glanced towards the hearth. 'There are no more logs in the basket,' he murmured. 'Can't have you getting cold. . . There's only one thing for it, as far as I can see.'

Standing up, he drew her to her feet, then, gathering her up into his arms, he turned and carried her towards the staircase in the corner of the room.

It was a bright frosty morning, the sun sparkling on the granite chips in the road and the steam rising from the radiator as Melanie drove her sister's car to the hospital.

They had agreed they would travel separately to work to avoid any speculation, for although they both felt like shouting their news from the frost-covered rooftops they also felt it only right that Peter and Sophie should be the first to know.

'Come for a meal tonight,' she had said as she kissed him before leaving the cottage, 'and we'll tell them together.'

It wasn't, however, easy to fool Donna. As they took their coffee break together she looked at Melanie and said, 'You look just like the cat that got the cream this morning—no prizes for guessing who's responsible. . .' Her gaze flickered to Gareth's office.

'Sshh, Donna, please,' Melanie protested. 'It's supposed to be a secret, for the time being at least.'

'Well, if that's the case you'd better do something about the stars in your eyes and tell Gareth to stop going around with a silly grin on his face,' Donna replied drily, then, her expression softening, she added, 'I'm so pleased for you both.'

'I'd forgotten what it was like to be so happy,' admitted Melanie with a sigh.

'Did you know Andrew's going home tomorrow?' asked Donna suddenly.

She nodded. 'Yes, Gareth and Dr Lineham have sorted it all out with Social Services. Andrew is going home to his mum, but will remain under the eye of the health visitor.'

'Do you think that will work out?' asked Donna doubtfully.

'We can only hope,' replied Melanie firmly. 'But I think what happened really shook his mother. I should imagine she would take better care of him in the future. She really didn't want him to go into care.'

Somehow Melanie got through the rest of the morning, but there seemed a sense of unreality about everything; then just as she finished changing the dressing of a little boy who'd had a hernia repair she heard Gareth call her name.

She looked up expectantly, her senses responding to the sound of his voice, her eyes eager to see the love reflected in his own. What she saw caused her heart to miss a beat.

'What is it?' She straightened up, moved away from the child's bed, and followed him into his office.

He turned to face her. 'Casualty have just phoned,' he said. 'You mustn't worry, Melanie; I'm sure it isn't anything. . .'

'The children. . .?' Her eyes widened in fear.

'It's Sophie. . .'

Her hand flew to her mouth. 'What is it? What's happened?'

'Apparently she's fallen off her bike. Your sister and Peter are with her.'

'I must go to her.'

'Of course. I'll come down with you. Donna, hol`
the fort here, will you? I'll be in Cas. if you need me.'

They took the lift down to Casualty, which was on
the ground floor, and as they were the only two in the
lift Gareth put his arms round Melanie and held her.

In spite of her anguish and uncertainty over what
she might find, she allowed herself briefly to lean
against him, relieved he was there with her, that she
didn't have to face alone whatever awaited her.

They were met in Casualty Reception by the house
officer.

'Hello, Mark.' Gareth took over. 'This is Melanie
Darby, one of my staff. We understand her young
daughter, Sophie, has been brought in.'

'That's right,' the doctor replied. 'She's just waiting
to go to X-ray. She had rather a nasty bump on her
head with a bit of concussion—we just want to make
sure there's no fracture of the cranium.'

'Where is she?' demanded Melanie. 'I want to see
her.'

'She's over there.' The SHO nodded across
Reception and Melanie hurried towards the cubicle
leaving Gareth to get more details.

She pulled aside the curtain, and the first thing she
saw was Jenny's strained expression, then Peter's
white face, then her gaze flew to her daughter, who
was lying on the couch.

'I fell off Cathie's bike; the path wath all frothty!'
Sophie exclaimed, then her eyes filled with tears and
she began to cry.

'Oh, Melanie, I'm sorry,' said Jenny. 'Honestly, I only took my eyes off her for a second.'

'That's right,' added Peter anxiously. 'It wasn't Aunty Jen's fault. The path was ever so slippery, and Cassie's bike is really too big for Sophie——'

'It's all right,' murmured Melanie. 'If it's anyone's fault, it's mine for not being there.'

'You can't help that,' sniffed Jenny. 'You have to work, and that's that.'

'Maybe that could all be about to change, at least for the time being,' said Melanie quietly as she kissed Sophie's tear-stained face. Before she could say more, Gareth suddenly appeared.

'What's this I hear about you practising for the Olympic cycling team?' he said to Sophie.

The little girl giggled, then turned her attention to the porter who had just arrived to take her to X-ray.

Sophie's X-rays were clear. The SHO said he wanted her to stay for a while under observation, then if all was well she could go home.

'You go on home, Jenny,' said Melanie to her sister. 'Your girls will be wondering where you've got to.'

'But how will you get home?' said Jenny anxiously.

'Don't worry about us; we'll get a taxi,' replied Melanie.

'They'll do nothing of the sort,' said Gareth firmly. 'I'll be taking them home.'

'Oh, well, in that case I'll go.' Jenny stood up and buttoned her coat, then she looked at Peter. 'Are you coming with me, Peter?'

He glanced from Gareth to Melanie, then shook h
head. 'No, I'll stay,' he said.

It was nearly dark when they finally got home, and
the windows of the houses in Winchester Close
twinkled with Christmas tree lights.

Gareth brought the jeep to a halt and glanced over
his shoulder to Melanie, who was sitting in the back
seat with Sophie on her lap.

'Is she all right?' he asked.

'Yes, she's fine.' Melanie kissed the top of her
daughter's head. 'I think she's been very lucky — she
could have been in hospital for Christmas. As it is,
we'll be all together now.'

Peter, who was sitting beside Gareth, suddenly
turned round. 'Are we going to Aunty Jen's on
Christmas Day, Mum?' he asked.

'No, Peter,' she replied. 'I hadn't told you before,
because I didn't want you to be disappointed, but
Aunty Jen is going out on Christmas Day. We shall
be at home on our own.'

In the silence that followed, Peter turned his head
to look at Gareth. 'What are you doing at Christmas?'
he asked.

'Well, I'm on duty Christmas Eve and Boxing
Day. . .' Gareth began.

'What about Christmas Day?' persisted Peter.

'Nothing really planned for Christmas Day,' Gareth
replied.

Melanie held her breath.

'Why don't you come to us?' said Peter gruffly.

'Would you like me to?'

'Oh, yeth,' said a sleepy voice from the back seat as Peter nodded and opened the door of the jeep.

Gareth came and helped Melanie and Sophie, and very briefly — so briefly that to anyone else it would have been imperceptible — Melanie allowed her eyes to meet his.

In the light from the overhead street-lamp she saw his smile, then they turned and followed Peter up the path to the house.

JANET DAILEY

A Collection

Three sensuous love stories from a world-class
author, bound together in one beautiful volume—
A Collection offers a unique chance for new fans to
sample some of Janet Dailey's earlier works and for
longtime readers to collect an edition to treasure.

Featuring:

THE IVORY CANE
REILLY'S WOMAN
STRANGE BEDFELLOW

Available from May   Priced £4.99

W☉RLDWIDE

LOVE ON CALL
4 FREE BOOKS AND 2 FREE GIFTS
FROM MILLS & BOON

Capture all the drama and emotion of a hectic medical world when you accept 4 Love on Call romances PLUS a cuddly teddy bear and a mystery gift - absolutely FREE and without obligation. And, if you choose, go on to enjoy 4 exciting Love on Call romances every month for only £1.80 each! Be sure to return the coupon below today to: Mills & Boon Reader Service, FREEPOST, PO Box 236, Croydon, Surrey CR9 9EL.

✂ — — — — — — — **NO STAMP REQUIRED** — — — — — — —

YES! Please rush me 4 FREE Love on Call books and 2 FREE gifts! Please also reserve me a Reader Service subscription, which means I can look forward to receiving 4 brand new Love on Call books for only £7.20 every month, postage and packing FREE. If I choose not to subscribe, I shall write to you within 10 days and still keep my FREE books and gifts. I may cancel or suspend my subscription at any time. I am over 18 years. Please write in BLOCK CAPITALS.

Ms/Mrs/Miss/Mr _____ **EP63D**

Address _____

_____

Postcode _____ Signature _____

mps
**MAILING
PREFERENCE
SERVICE**

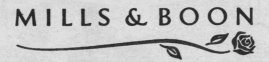

MILLS & BOON

LOVE ON CALL

The books for enjoyment this month are:

VET IN A QUANDARY Mary Bowring
NO SHADOW OF DOUBT Abigail Gordon
PRIORITY CARE Mary Hawkins
TO LOVE AGAIN Laura MacDonald

♥   ♥   ♥   ♥   ♥

Treats in store!

Watch next month for the following absorbing stories:

A MAN OF HONOUR Caroline Anderson
RUNNING AWAY Lilian Darcy
THE FRAGILE HEART Jean Evans
THE SENIOR PARTNER'S DAUGHTER Elizabeth Harrison

Available from W.H. Smith, John Menzies, Volume One, Forbuoys, Martins, Tesco, Asda, Safeway and other paperback stockists.

Also available from Mills & Boon Reader Service, Freepost, P.O. Box 236, Croydon, Surrey CR9 9EL.

Readers in South Africa - write to:
Book Services International Ltd, P.O. Box 41654, Craighall, Transvaal 2024.